BOOKS 1—3

Lily to the Rescue
Lily to the Rescue: Two Little Piggies
Lily to the Rescue: The Not-So-Stinky Skunk

ALSO BY W. BRUCE CAMERON

Bailey's Story

Bella's Story

Cooper's Story

Ellie's Story

Lacey's Story

Lily's Story

Max's Story

Molly's Story

Shelby's Story

Toby's Story

Lily to the Rescue

Lily to the Rescue: Two Little Piggies

Lily to the Rescue: The Not-So-Stinky Skunk

Lily to the Rescue: Dog Dog Goose

Lily to the Rescue: Lost Little Leopard

Lily to the Rescue: The Misfit Donkey

Lily to the Rescue: Foxes in a Fix

Lily to the Rescue: The Three Bears

W. BRUCE CAMERON

LILY
TO THE rescue

BOOKS 1—3

Lily to the Rescue
Lily to the Rescue: Two Little Piggies
Lily to the Rescue: The Not-So-Stinky Skunk

Illustrations by
JENNIFER L. MEYER

A TOM DOHERTY ASSOCIATES BOOK
NEW YORK

LILY TO THE RESCUE BIND-UP BOOKS 1—3: LILY TO THE RESCUE, TWO LITTLE PIGGIES, AND THE NOT-SO-STINKY SKUNK

Lily to the Rescue copyright © 2020 by W. Bruce Cameron
Lily to the Rescue: Two Little Piggies copyright © 2020 by W. Bruce Cameron
Lily to the Rescue: The Not-So-Stinky Skunk copyright © 2020 by W. Bruce Cameron

Illustrations © 2020 by Jennifer L. Meyer

A Starscape Book
Published by Tom Doherty Associates
120 Broadway
New York, NY 10271

www.tor-forge.com

ISBN 978-1-250-86765-0 (trade paperback)

Our books may be purchased in bulk for promotional, educational, or business use. Please contact your local bookseller or the Macmillan Corporate and Premium Sales Department at 1-800-221-7945, extension 5442, or by email at MacmillanSpecialMarkets@macmillan.com.

First Edition: 2022

Printed in the United States of America

0   9   8   7   6   5   4   3   2   1

Contents

Dedicated to my dog Tucker,

who loves his tiny piece of cheese.

M y name is Lily, and I have a lot of friends.

My best friend of all, of course, is Maggie Rose.

In the nighttime, I sleep on Maggie Rose's bed, pressed up against her warm legs. I get to lie there until Mom or Dad pokes a head in the doorway and says the word *school*.

Maggie Rose will groan a little, and then she climbs slowly out of bed and puts on her

clothes and goes into the kitchen for breakfast with her brothers. While she's chang-
ing clothes, I lie on the bed, missing her legs
and trying to show her that we would all be
happier if she just climbed back under the
covers.

But she never does that on days people say
school. I don't know why.

I think school must be a place, because
one day when Mom said *school*, Maggie Rose

let me ride in the back seat of the car with her. We went to a room with many children her age sitting in chairs. I sat next to Maggie Rose at the front of the room so that everyone could admire what a good dog I could be. I am very good at sitting.

Maggie Rose said, "Hello. My name is Maggie Rose Murphy. I live in Golden,

Colorado. I am in the third grade. My father is a game warden for the state of Colorado, and my mother works in animal rescue. She's a veterinarian. My dog's name is Lily."

When she said my name, I looked up at Maggie Rose and wagged. I did not know what we were doing, but all the children were looking at us, and it made me feel very important.

"Lily is a rescue dog for two reasons," Maggie Rose continued. I wagged again. "The first reason is that she was taken in by the shelter where my mom works, so she was rescued. And the second reason is that most days she goes back to the shelter to take care of all the animals there."

Maggie Rose started smiling and speaking a little more quickly. "Lily plays with the other dogs and helps them relax and not feel scared. She plays with the cats, too. She loves cats! Sometimes she curls up with the kittens and they sleep together. It helps because then the kittens don't grow up to be scared of dogs, and they can get adopted into families with dogs."

She paused and took a deep breath.

"So Lily has a job—a job in animal rescue. On weekends, I sometimes help at the

shelter, too. It's good for the puppies or kittens to get used to kids. Then they're not nervous around us."

"Lucky!" one of the children moaned.

I wagged some more. It just seemed like a good idea.

"I have two brothers," Maggie Rose went on. "One is named Bryan, and he is in fifth grade. One is named Craig, and he is in eighth grade. When I grow up, I want to be a veterinarian. When Craig grows up, he wants to be a baseball player. And I don't think Bryan will ever grow up."

For some reason, all the children laughed when Maggie Rose said this even though I had not done anything special. Sometimes people laugh just because they are happy there is a dog in the room.

"My name is Maggie Rose Murphy, and that is my report," Maggie Rose said. Everyone clapped because I was doing such a good job doing Sit. Then all the children lined up and took turns petting me, which was very nice. Maggie Rose gave me a treat, and that was even nicer.

That was an unusual day. On most days when somebody says *school*, I don't get to go to that place with all the children and the treats. Instead, Maggie Rose leaves after breakfast, and I go to Work.

Work is a place just like school is a place. I go there with Mom. There are good treats at Work, and there are also friends: dogs, cats, and other animals in cages. The dogs and cats and the rest of the animals stay at Work for a while and then leave with happy people. I am the only dog who goes to Work and then goes home and goes back again the next day. That makes me special.

I like Work days, even though Maggie Rose gets out of bed before I am ready for her to do that. But the days when nobody says *school* and when I don't go to Work are even better.

Then I can spend the whole day with my girl, Maggie Rose. And sometimes we go to the dog park!

The dog park is the most wonderful place I have ever been. Even better than bed with Maggie Rose's warm legs. Even better than Work, where there are friends and treats.

At the dog park, there are dogs, squirrels, birds, and children. I do not know if all the dogs are there all the time or if they just make sure to be there when I arrive.

I am friends with every-
one at the dog park, except
the squirrels. It really isn't
possible to make friends with
squirrels, because they always
run away. I have tried, and it just
doesn't work.

One day at the dog park, I made a
new friend.

There are some important rules in the dog park. First, one dog should never take a toy away from another dog. Dogs don't like that. People can take away toys if they want, because they are people. The rule doesn't apply to people.

Next, a dog should always politely sniff another dog in the butt. If you don't sniff a dog, it is considered to be very rude. (This rule does not apply to people, either.)

When Maggie Rose first lets me into the dog park, I love to run and run and run. I will wag and bow and sniff all my friends, and I will chase any dog who looks like he or she needs a good chasing.

Most of the other dogs in the park run after the squirrels, but I don't because we have had many different kinds of squirrels at Work, and I have learned they don't like to be chased. That makes no sense, but squirrels are squirrels and not dogs. Cats don't like to be chased, either, so they may be a type of squirrel. I'm not sure about that, though.

Being chased, or chasing, is one of the most fun times to be had, and it is not my fault if squirrels and cats don't understand this.

After chasing, I usually go over to the water bowl to get a drink. There is an enormous water bowl at the dog park for all of us to share. One time a dog named Boggs sat in the water dish. He is a big dog with a black face. I do not know why he thought he would be comfortable sitting in the water bowl, but once he did, the water smelled like Boggs and no one wanted to take a drink of it.

Fortunately, Maggie Rose came over and put in fresh water, so we didn't have to drink Boggs-water. We were all grateful for this, but we were nervous that Boggs might sit in the nice new water.

We tried to distract him by going over to the trees on the other side of the park where the male dogs lift their legs and the females squat. At least, that's why I went and squatted there, so that Boggs would be lured to come over to examine the fresh scent. The other dogs may just have marked the area because I was doing it.

Anyway, it succeeded, because Boggs naturally needed to spend a lot of time sniffing all the trees and lifting his own leg, and then he had to leave with his person so he didn't have a chance to put his butt in the water bowl again.

I suppose people can sit in water bowls if they want, but I have never seen anyone do it. I've never seen any dog but Boggs do it, either. And he's an odd animal, anyway, because he never runs after a ball—not when it is thrown by a person, not when another dog has it in his mouth. He may not understand what a ball even is.

On the day that I made a new friend, I was in the far end of the dog park by myself. I like to go there sometimes and think about what a wonderful life I have. I get to go to Work. I get to play with all sorts of animals. There's the dog park and Maggie Rose. No one has a better life than I do.

Running along the back of the dog park, there is a fence that I can see through. Overhead, there are many trees that drop nuts on the ground. At the base of one of the trees, I saw a little squirrel. I knew that Maggie Rose called that kind of squirrel a *chipmunk*, but it sure looked like a squirrel to me. It hopped like a squirrel, ate nuts like a squirrel, and it certainly smelled like a squirrel. People make all the rules and can name things whatever they want, but to me, a squirrel is a squirrel is a squirrel.

The chipmunk was busy finding nuts and stuffing them into its mouth. There were so many nuts in there that its cheeks were puffed out in a very silly fashion. No dog would do something so silly, but squirrels have different rules—for one thing, they are allowed to climb trees. (I don't really like nuts. Some dogs do, but to me it's squirrel food. I would much rather have a meat treat.)

This chipmunk was so busy making silly cheeks with his nuts that he did not notice that there was a large hawk circling overhead.

At once, I became very concerned. I knew from doing work high up in the mountains with Dad that a hawk hunts lit-tle animals. I had seen hawks fly down and grab small crea-tures the

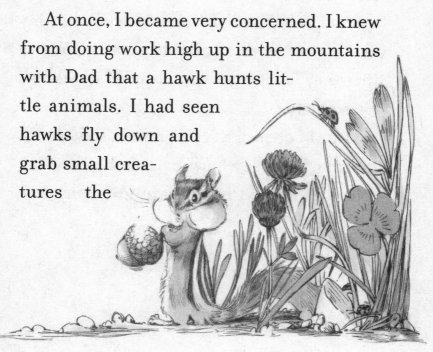

size of a chipmunk. Was this hawk flying around and around the little chipmunk because it was planning to hunt it?

I could not let that happen. Because the chipmunk was in the dog park, it was one of my friends. Maybe not a friend who would chase a ball or wrestle with a stick, but a friend just the same. I could not let the hawk hunt a friend.

But how could I stop it from doing that? Dogs cannot fly any more than we can climb trees. I wondered if I should bark, but my experience with squirrels of all kinds is that they don't care what dogs do unless we chase them.

But if I chased the chipmunk, that would not help because a hawk can catch a running creature. I stood frozen, afraid for my new little friend.

I was still watching the chipmunk and seeing that the hawk was coming closer and closer when suddenly the sky darkened, and I heard the flutter of many wings. It was a big mob of crows! They were all flying straight at the hawk!

It was just like when Bryan and Craig played football, which is a game where children run around with a ball and dogs are not allowed to help, even though putting in a dog or two would make it much more fun. I had learned from watching football that when a child is carrying the ball, the other kids will all chase him and jump on him. That's what the crows were doing now. They were swooping down and trying to grab the hawk with their beaks!

The hawk was clearly annoyed by all these big black birds that were flying around and pushing it and getting in its way. For some reason, the crows were trying to make the hawk fly away from the dog park and go somewhere else. Maybe there was a hawk park.

The hawk swooped and dove and changed direction, but there were so many crows pestering it, it finally gave up and flew away. The little chipmunk was safe!

Not that it was paying any attention. It was so busy digging for nuts, it had never once bothered to look up at the sky. That's just one of the many differences between squirrels and dogs: a dog always knows what is going on.

When the crows finally succeeded in driving away the hawk, the sky was clear of any birds. And that is when I saw Casey.

I did not know Casey's name at the time, of course. That would come later. All I knew was that I saw a crow hopping very strangely on the ground. One wing flapped, but the other one seemed pinched and pressed up against his side. There was something wrong with the crow, because they are supposed to fly, and this one could not.

Helping animals that cannot do what they are supposed to do is the most important thing that Mom and Dad do at Work. Sometimes we help animals who are lost and hungry and just need a warm place and a good dinner before their family comes to get them. Sometimes the animals are hurt and need different kinds of help.

This crow seemed hurt.

I turned and looked across the dog park. Maggie Rose had been sitting on a bench reading a book, but now she was standing and looking at me. Maggie Rose is my person, and she can tell when I am upset.

I turned back to see what the crow was doing and noticed something amazing. The little chipmunk was hopping around with so many nuts in its mouth that they were falling out of its cheeks! I guess chipmunks love making silly faces so much, they will keep stuffing nuts into their mouths until they are nearly ready to burst.

As I watched, I saw the little chipmunk scamper over to a hole under the fence and drop a couple of nuts on the way. That is when the amazing thing happened: the crow with the broken wing hopped over to the nuts, picked them up, and ate them.

I had found out a new thing: crows and chipmunks were friends! This made me happy. I like to make animal friends, too, but I don't eat nuts, so I did not go over to join in the shared meal.

I turned back to my girl and saw that she was coming toward me with a frown on her face. She saw the crow and put a hand to her mouth.

"Lily," she called, "what happened to that crow? Is it hurt?"

I wagged and sat, waiting for her to come help the poor bird. She approached slowly, so I knew that she didn't want to frighten the crow.

Now Maggie Rose was standing beside me. She knelt down and petted my head. "Good dog, Lily. That poor crow has a broken wing!" Maggie Rose held my head in her hand and looked into my eyes. "Lily," she said, "I'll go get Mom. You stay here and guard the crow. Watch him, Lily! Keep the crow safe!"

I did not know what Maggie Rose was saying, but I could hear concern in her voice, and I knew it had something to do with the poor crow. Also, she had said the word *Mom*, and I thought maybe what she was saying was that we needed Mom here to help with the crow and then later give me some treats from her pocket. Mom often had treats.

I was surprised when Maggie Rose turned and ran away. Did she want me to chase her? But the crow was clearly in trouble.

Maggie Rose passed through the double gate to the dog park and ran down the street toward Work. Where was she going? What was going to happen now? Why hadn't she taken me with her?

But I knew she would be back. Maggie Rose always came back, no matter what. While I was waiting for her, I decided I should make friends with the crow whose wing did not work.

I moved closer to him, but when I took a step, the crow hopped away. I took another step, and the crow hopped again. Even though

I am a friendly dog and everyone loves me, this crow seemed afraid of me.

This was ridiculous, of course. Cats are not afraid of me, horses are not afraid of me, and dogs are certainly not afraid of me. Even the little chipmunk hadn't been afraid—it had been so busy stuffing its face that it had paid me no attention at all. But this crow seemed to think I would hurt him.

With every hop, the crow was closer to the fence. When he reached the fence, I think he felt trapped. He turned and looked at me.

Now, if I went closer, the crow would have nowhere to hop. It would feel like being in a cage.

I decided that the best thing I could do was stop trying to catch up to the crow, just lie down and watch it. Maybe that way it would understand that I was Lily, a very nice dog who had many friends who were not dogs: cats, a ferret, kittens, and even a bunny rabbit.

Now that I was lying down with my nose pointed toward the crow, he was looking at me very closely. He kept turning his head one way and then the other.

I waited patiently, thinking this would be what Maggie Rose would want. She had never left me alone in the dog park before, so I figured out that I should not do what I usually did—chase other dogs and make sure that Boggs didn't sit in the water dish. Instead, I would watch this crow.

After some time of just staring at me, the crow with the broken wing took a hop in my direction! I decided it was a very young crow. It wasn't a baby, but it seemed smaller and somehow smoother than a lot of crows I had seen in the park.

The crow took another hop, then stopped

and twisted his head. I waited. The crow took another hop. Clearly, he wasn't just afraid—he also wanted to understand what I was doing there, just lying in the grass, not moving. Well, if it made him feel calm and curious, I was prepared to lie there all day.

The crow took another hop.

I waited.

With every hop, the crow flapped one wing, but the other one remained completely still, hanging by its side.

The crow took another hop. Another. And then, suddenly, the crow jumped up and landed right on my back!

Well, this was certainly a strange day. I had never seen a chipmunk feed a crow before. I had never seen a flock of crows save a chipmunk from a hawk before. I had never been left alone in the dog park before. And now, I had a crow on my back—something else that had never happened before.

When a crow is on a dog's back, the dog cannot easily fall asleep. However, the sun was warm, and I felt myself getting drowsy. Would Maggie Rose mind if I took a little nap while I was waiting for her?

My eyes may have shut, but they snapped open when I smelled something familiar. It was Maggie Rose! And it was the smell of Mom and Dad, too. They must have entered the dog park and were probably coming toward me because their scents were growing stronger.

I wagged, aware that I still had a crow on my back so I couldn't stand up and turn to face my human family. I hoped they would not think that I was being a bad dog. It was certainly a little embarrassing.

"Good dog, Lily!" I heard Maggie Rose call. That made it all right.

At the sound of my girl's voice, the crow jumped off my back and hopped back over to the fence, where it felt safe. Since I was back to being a regular dog and was no longer a crow bed, I stood up, shook, and ran to my girl and Mom and Dad.

Dad was carrying something that looked like a big handful of thin cloth. "It does look like a broken wing," he said. "We'll have to take him in and see if he can be saved."

"If he can be saved?" Maggie Rose repeated. "What do you mean, *if?*" I looked at her in concern. She sounded shocked.

"Well," Dad replied, "when a wild bird breaks a wing, it can be hard to repair. And this is a young crow, and crows are very social birds. I worry about keeping him at the shelter while he heals."

"What does it mean if we can't help him?" Maggie Rose wanted to know.

Dad was quiet for a moment. "Maggie Rose, we'll do what we can, but a bird with a broken wing can't survive in the wild. We'd have to keep him in a cage. I don't think he would be happy."

"But, Dad," Maggie Rose cried, "then we have to save him! He and Lily are friends! He was standing on Lily's back!"

"Well," Dad said, "we have to catch him first."

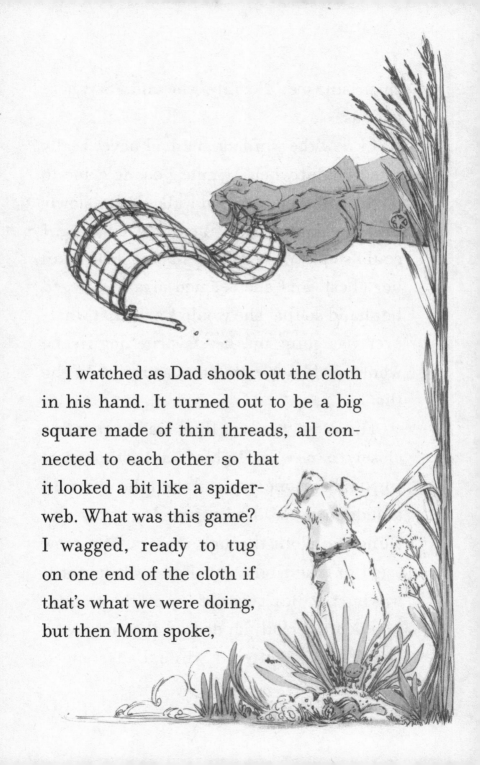

I watched as Dad shook out the cloth in his hand. It turned out to be a big square made of thin threads, all connected to each other so that it looked a bit like a spider-web. What was this game? I wagged, ready to tug on one end of the cloth if that's what we were doing, but then Mom spoke, surprising me. "No, Lily," she said. "Stay here with us."

I knew the word *no* and had never really liked it. But when Maggie Rose told me to do Sit, I obeyed her. Dad walked very slowly toward the crow with the damaged wing. I could sense Maggie Rose's heart beating in her chest, and she seemed afraid. I nosed her hand so that she would know that whatever was going on, her favorite dog in the whole world was right here, so it couldn't be that bad.

The crow was watching Dad even more closely than I was. The bird was back to twisting his head one way and then the other. In a sudden move, Dad raised his arms and flung the cloth through the air. The crow tried to take flight, but I guess it forgot it was hurt. It didn't even lift up off the ground.

Then the cloth landed on the crow, who flapped and fluttered while Dad stepped forward and grabbed the cloth and cinched it shut.

The crow squawked then, and I was sad because the squawk sounded so sad. Clearly, the crow thought something really bad was happening. I stopped doing Sit and went over to sniff at the cloth to try to make the crow feel better, but I could tell that it did not help.

Dad very carefully lifted the cloth, examining the crow. Mom walked over to look, too. Maggie Rose, however, came to me and rubbed her open hand on my head. "You are a good dog, Lily," she said. "You kept the crow calm."

I wagged at being a good dog for Maggie Rose.

"What is that around his wing?" Mom asked Dad.

Dad was tenderly turning the crow inside the cloth. "It looks like some sort of wire or string. It's so tight it's cut his flesh; can you see? I'm not sure what it is, but there are all sorts of wires and kite strings in the trees that a bird can get tangled in."

"Let's get this crow back to the rescue and see what we can do for the poor thing," Mom said.

When we arrived at Work, Dad carried the crow into a room, and I trotted off to see several of my newest friends. There were three little kittens in a cage I could not reach who were delighted to stand and stare down at me. They wanted to play, I knew, because on other days, Maggie Rose had let them out and we'd scampered around the room with each other. But today she did not do that.

Farther down the row of cages, right on the floor, there was an old dog named Brewster who thumped his tail but did not get up to greet me. Brewster was a brown, lazy dog who liked to take naps. He had been at Work longer than any other animal. Mom

sometimes called him a *senior dog,* which I suppose meant the same as *good dog* because Brewster was allowed to stay at Work so long.

"Brewster," Mom would say, "is going to be a challenge to adopt out. People want puppies more than they want senior dogs." I did not know what she was saying, but hearing her say *puppies* and *dogs* made me happy.

Brewster and I sometimes played together out in the yard, and one time we went to the dog park together, but for the most part, Brewster really liked to focus his attention on sleeping.

I greeted the other dogs and the adult cats in their cages and then went to be with Maggie Rose.

"Oh, Lily," Maggie Rose said, holding me tightly, "I sure hope Mom and Dad can save that poor bird."

The next time I saw that bird, he had a name and an outfit!

Maggie Rose and I went into Work a few days after I'd met the crow at the dog park. I smelled him right away, and Maggie Rose called out to him. "Good morning, Casey," she sang. "How's your wing today?"

Casey lived in a big wire cage with seeds on the floor and a stick he could hop on, sort of like a tree but with no leaves. He did not

have a blanket to sleep on, which might be why I never saw him lying down.

"Mom," Maggie Rose asked, "when will Casey be able to fly again?"

When she asked this question, Maggie Rose had been training me to do Roll Over. Roll Over is a complicated trick where a dog lies down on her stomach as if to take a nap like old Brewster. Then she lies on her back as if to get a tummy rub, and then she flops to the other side. I thought it was pretty pointless, but when I did Roll Over, Maggie

Rose gave me a turkey treat. I will do pretty much anything for turkey, pointless or not.

Mom was carrying a cat who had just arrived the day before. The cat was purring, which is what cats do instead of barking.

"Well, honey," Mom said, "we'll have to see if the operation was successful. If it was, then there's no reason why Casey shouldn't fly again. But we had to deal with some pretty deep cuts. We'll just have to wait."

I could feel that Maggie Rose was sad, so I went to comfort her by doing Roll Over without being asked. For some reason, there was no turkey for this.

With people, the rules change all the time. Casey's outfit was a white coat that he wore on the wing he had been dragging. It smelled like cloth and a little bit like a strong chemical. His other wing still fluttered and stuck out, but he seemed to like wearing his new coat so much he never moved that wing at all. He let me sniff the coat, but I honestly didn't find it very interesting.

Casey and I were becoming good friends. I would visit him by going to his cage and sticking my nose against the wires every day. Casey would hop over to greet me.

One day, I noticed Casey watching Mom as she opened the cage door to put seeds in a bowl for him. After Mom had left, Casey went to the door of his cage and began pecking at it with his black beak. With a little bit of a rattle, the door swung open! Casey hopped out.

I bowed and wagged and jumped around in excitement as Casey hopped along the floor between the stacks of cages, saying hello to all the animals.

Casey was happy to see Brewster, who actually roused himself from a nap to wander over and sniff Casey from the other side of his gate. But Casey was far more interested in the kittens than anything else. He hopped up from one cage to another on the stack until he was off the floor, out of my reach, standing on top of an empty cage so that he could look right into the one with the three little kittens inside.

The kittens tried to reach out to play with Casey. They could stick their soft little paws between the wires to bat at him, but Casey was not interested in having them pet him on the head like a person would pet a dog.

Casey seemed to understand that kittens are not dogs, which is good information to have. A dog knows how to play by chewing very gently on a playmate, but kittens play with their claws. Sometimes they can accidentally hurt you. Adult cats are even more iffy when it comes to playing—some of them like dogs, and some of them despise dogs.

This makes no sense because dogs are wonderful, but it is true, just like it's true

that you Should Not Sit in the Dog Park Water Bowl. Casey was showing the proper amount of caution around the kittens, I felt.

When he made his way back down, one wing fluttering, he jumped right up on my back for a dog ride. I walked him around the room so he could see everything there was to see.

At first, it felt very strange to have a big black bird on my back, his tiny feet gripping my fur. But soon it started to feel ordinary. Casey liked to be up there—I think it made him feel safe. And I liked to have him up there because it was a completely new way of playing with another animal.

After taking a tour of all the cages, Casey hopped back up into his cage and then, reaching out with his beak, he pulled the door to his cage shut. I was very impressed.

We did this every day that I went to Work. Most days I was at Work because Mom or Dad had said the word *school,* and that meant Maggie Rose was gone for some time. Other days, though—the best days—were when Maggie Rose came to Work with me!

She would play with the kittens, she would play with Brewster, she would play with any puppies, and she would even reach her hand into Casey's cage, and he would hop onto her wrist and she would pull him out and talk to him.

One day, Mom came into the room while Maggie Rose was holding Casey. "Mom,"

Maggie Rose asked, "how is Casey's wing doing? Is it going to heal okay?"

"Well," Mom said, "we'll take his bandage off in another few days, and then we'll see."

"What'll happen if the wing didn't get fixed?" Maggie Rose asked.

"Oh," Mom said sadly, "I'm sure we'll figure out a home for Casey. But I think he'd rather be able to fly."

"I'd love to fly. Would you like to fly, Lily?"

I wagged, not sure what we were talking about but ready to play any game Maggie Rose came up with.

The next day when no one said *school,* Maggie Rose came to Work and watched while Mom removed Casey's coat. For the first time since I had met him, Casey flapped both of his wings! He didn't fly, though. He just sort of stretched his wings out.

Then Casey hopped down onto the floor and went over to visit the kittens.

"We still don't know if Casey can fly or not," said Mom. "Let's take him outside."

We all went into the yard together, and Dad came out to join us. I was happy that Casey was outside for the first time since he had come to live with us, because there are toys and grass and sticks out in the yard. I wondered what sort of games we might play together.

peck peck

I hoped if I grabbed a ball Casey would do Chase-Me. That's a great game because I have the ball and everyone else wants it. Maggie Rose's brothers, Bryan and Craig, often played Chase-Me. But sometimes Craig was able to catch me and grab the ball, and then I had to play Chase-Craig, which wasn't as fun.

Casey hopped on the ground and poked a little at the dirt. I went and found a rope toy to see if he was interested in tugging on it, but he mostly just wanted to jump around.

"Can't he remember how to fly?" Maggie Rose asked anxiously, looking up at Mom.

Mom shook her head. "I don't know, honey. His wing may still be feeling sore or weak. I'm just not sure."

I felt the sadness coming off Mom and wondered if I should take the rope toy to her

to make her happy. Then Maggie Rose held out her hand, kneeling next to Casey. Casey hopped right up onto her hand. "Come on, Casey. You can fly," she urged.

Maggie Rose held Casey out at the end of her arm, but nothing else happened. I sat and scratched behind my ear, thinking that crow games are very different from dog games.

"Please, Casey. Please try to fly!"

Casey lifted his wings a little, and I stared at my girl, Maggie Rose, because both Casey and I could hear in her voice that this was important.

Crows can fly, and come together to mob hawks to protect their chipmunk friends, and hop over to see kittens. But as far as I know, they can't do much else. A dog, now—a dog can do a great many wonderful things if it just understands what is needed.

I decided that since Maggie Rose was holding her arm out, I should lift my paw, which is called *Shake*. It is a trick that Bryan taught me. He had hamburger pieces, so I caught on right away.

But nobody seemed to notice my Shake, even though I was doing it so well.

"I know," Mom said. "Maggie Rose, why don't you try running? Maybe the feeling of movement will give Casey the idea that he should try flying."

"That's a good idea," Dad agreed. "Maggie Rose? Keep your arm out and run into the wind."

I was startled and thrilled when all of a sudden Maggie Rose started to run, Casey still perched on her hand. Casey seemed excited, too, because he raised his wings. Maggie Rose ran around and around the yard. I chased her, holding the rope toy in my mouth so that this new game would be even more fun.

With a squawk, Casey flapped his wings. With a gasp of delight, Maggie Rose lifted her hand even higher. Casey flew into the air!

"Look, Dad!" Maggie Rose shouted. "Casey's flying!"

I sat with the rope toy in my mouth and watched as Casey soared far up into the sky. He flew in a big circle, flapping his

wings. Maggie Rose was clapping, and Mom and Dad were smiling. Then Casey came gliding out of the sky and landed at Maggie Rose's feet.

I barked excitedly, dropping the rope toy in the grass. Then I jumped on it. We were all having such fun!

Dad turned to Mom. "Oh, boy," he said. "This isn't good."

Just like that, the joy left my human family, even though I was shaking that rope toy like crazy.

I hoped Casey understood what was going on, because I sure didn't.

That evening, I lay under Bryan's feet at the dinner table. Bryan will sometimes hand down a piece of dinner for me to snack on while I am lying there, waiting for everyone to finish and practically fainting with all the wonderful smells. Maggie Rose is my girl, but Bryan and Craig are part of the family, too,

so I love all of them. I love Bryan a lot if he is eating.

"I'm worried that Casey's become domesticated," Dad said. "That doesn't often happen with young birds, but he didn't seem to want to fly off. Maybe he's gotten too dependent on us giving him food."

"Maybe he just needs to find a crow family," Mom said.

"Yeah," Craig agreed, "like playing soccer. You can play by yourself, but it's much more fun with a team."

"Well," Bryan replied, "not more fun for Maggie Rose. She's such a little runt that no team would want her."

"That's just not a very nice thing to say, Bryan," Dad replied gruffly. "I think maybe after you apologize to Maggie Rose you should do the dishes for the rest of the week so you can think about what it would take for you to be nicer to your sister."

Bryan groaned and kicked his legs and did not feed me any more treats.

"Maggie Rose, you are such fun. Would you like to play ball with me after dinner?" Craig asked sweetly.

"Yes!" my girl said.

I jumped up. Ball?

Dad laughed. "Okay, that sounded pretty fake, Craig."

Then everyone laughed.

Except Bryan.

The next day was not a day where people said *school*. Instead, we went for a car ride! Dad drove, and Craig sat next to him. Casey was in his cage in the very back, and I was in the second seat with Maggie Rose and Bryan. The three of us in the second seat were mostly watching out the window for other dogs to bark at.

"Wouldn't it make more sense to release Casey up in the mountains?" Maggie Rose asked. "There are lots of crows up there."

"Good question, Maggie Rose," Dad answered. "But a flock of crows in the mountains is much less likely to accept a strange crow than a flock in the city. No one knows why, but I suspect it has to do with the birds all being more crowded here. The crows in cities are much more used to seeing strange birds. So we're going to take Casey to a big city park where I know there are lots and lots of crows hanging around, and I hope they accept him."

"But what if they don't like Casey?"

"Well, we can keep trying. Maybe we'll find another flock. Or Casey might just fly off on his own. Lone crows are not uncommon, especially males, but they're always safer in a group. Do you know what a flock of crows is called?"

"I know!" Craig called out.

"Let's see if your sister or brother knows," Dad replied.

Bryan rubbed his chin. "A crow flock?"

Dad laughed.

"I don't know," Maggie Rose admitted.

I saw a squirrel out the window and wagged.

"Craig?"

"A murder?" Craig replied.

Bryan laughed.

"Actually," Dad replied, "Craig is right.

A group of crows is called a *murder* of crows. No one's sure why. Maybe just because they'll surround a dead animal to eat it. But there are people who think that crows are evil and bring death."

"Casey isn't evil," Maggie Rose objected. "He's friendly!"

"I did a report on crows," Craig said. "They're smart. When a crow dies, the other crows will all surround him, because they're trying to figure out what happened. If it was an animal attack, they try to learn from it."

"Even I didn't know that," Dad said. "Very interesting. And that's another reason why it would be better if Casey joined a family— so that he could learn from them."

We went to a park! It was not the kind of park where dogs are allowed to run around without a leash. That made it not the best kind of park, but still, there were many smells and there were trees and there was a big pond—and I noticed there were a lot of birds.

There were big birds floating in the water, and there were little birds in the trees, and there were groups of crows that were on the ground poking at the dirt with their beaks. Dad set Casey's cage on the ground, and Casey was so excited he opened the door himself and jumped out.

"Wow!" Dad said. "I didn't know Casey knew how to do that!"

"You're a smart bird, Casey!" Maggie Rose called out.

Casey was obviously very interested in the crows that were across a big lawn. He kept looking at them, cocking his head to one side and the other, the way he had done when he first met me. After a time, he hopped up and flew a little bit closer to the big group of crows. They ignored Casey, probably not realizing what a special bird he was and that he had a dog for a friend.

Maggie Rose and Dad walked around pointing at birds, and Bryan and Craig threw a ball to each other. I decided to stick with the boys, and sure enough, Bryan dropped one of Craig's throws, and then we had a lot of fun playing Chase-Me-I-Have-Bryan's-Ball-and-You-Don't. Craig and Bryan kept yelling, "Drop it, Lily!" which I decided meant "Keep running with the ball, Lily!"

Eventually, I let the boys tackle me and take the ball out of my mouth. "Yuck," Craig said, "it's covered in dog spit!"

I wagged at the word *dog*. I trotted over to be with Dad and Maggie Rose because they were down at the pond watching the big birds float.

After a little while, I noticed that Casey had hopped closer and closer to the other crows. I wondered if he was making friends with them. I wondered if they would let me make friends, too.

The trouble was, I did not know any crow games other than the one where Casey would ride on my back. There were many, many crows, and I did not think I could hold all of them up on my back.

Then I saw a dog running across the park. It was a brown spotted dog who was dragging his leash.

"A springer spaniel," Dad said to Maggie Rose. "That's a bird dog. Bred to hunt birds with his owner. See how excited he is with all the birds in the park? He probably yanked the leash right out of his owner's hand."

I watched as the brown dog very rudely ran right into the middle of Casey's friends. They all took off into the air, Casey included.

They flew around the park in a big, open circle. And then they flew up into the air over the trees and went away.

"Beau! Come back here!" a woman was yelling. She had her hands on her hips, but the brown spotted dog didn't seem to know that meant he was being a bad dog. I knew, though, so I pressed against Maggie Rose's leg, being a good dog, and waited for Casey to return.

But Casey did not come back.

Dad called the boys, and we all went to the car. I noticed Maggie Rose had her head down, as if she were watching for something to happen on the ground.

When we got to the car, Casey was not in his cage. I realized then that he was going to stay with his crow friends. Maybe they would all find some chipmunks to play with.

I was very sad. Maggie Rose was my best friend in the world, but Casey was my best bird friend. I had not realized how much I enjoyed being with Casey until he left.

"I know you were sorry to see Casey go," Dad said to my girl. "But believe me, this is best. It's your mom's job and mine, too. We take care of animals, we help them get better when they're sick or injured, and then we release them back into the wild."

"Except puppies," Craig said.

"Right," Dad replied. "Dogs can't live in the wild, so your mom finds them homes."

"And cats," Bryan said.

"True enough."

"And monkeys!" Craig said. He laughed.

"Whales! Dolphins!" Bryan hooted.

"If I come across a whale up in the mountains, I will do my best to find it a good home." Dad chuckled.

Both boys were laughing, but Maggie Rose was sad. She could probably feel the emptiness in the cage behind us, just as I did. It felt as if Casey were still in there, but every time I checked, he wasn't. Casey was gone.

I hoped Casey would be happy with his new friends. But I was sure he would miss me, just the way I was missing him.

We went back to Work, and I took a nap with Brewster out in the yard while Maggie Rose helped Mom with the cat cages. I had a dream that Casey was on my back. Then I went in and took a nap with Maggie Rose on a narrow, soft bed where she liked to lie down sometimes, often with a book. She was still a sad girl, so I pressed up against her, letting her know that she had the love of her dog.

I was sound asleep when I heard a tap. I opened one lazy eye, wondering what I had just heard. Then there was another tap. This was certainly a puzzle. What could be making that noise? Should I get up and see what was going on, or nap?

Nap, I decided.

Tap.

I raised my head and looked around. Was someone knocking on the door? I did not think that was it. I yawned and started to put my head back down and heard it again. *Tap. Tap, tap.*

All right, time to figure out what was happening. I stretched, but I stayed on the bed so that another nap could be easily had if I decided whatever was making the noise wasn't worth investigating.

Tap.

I looked and saw to my surprise that a crow was standing on the window ledge,

tapping on the glass with his beak. It was
Casey! He was back!

Tap.

Maggie Rose seemed to be sound asleep, so I gave her face a lick. She kept her eyes closed but wiped at her cheek with her fingers. I licked her again. Giggling, she opened her eyes.

"Oh, Lily, you are so silly. Why are you kissing me right now?"

Tap.

Maggie Rose heard the noise. She sat up and frowned. Then her face brightened, and she gasped. "Look, Lily! It's Casey!"

We ran down the hallway and out the door into the yard. Casey was waiting for us. I circled the yard joyously while Casey flew over and landed right on Maggie Rose's outstretched hand. "Why are you here, Casey?" she asked. "Didn't you want to stay with your new crow family?"

Casey twisted his head back and forth at Maggie Rose's question, so maybe he understood it. Then he lifted his wings and flapped up into the air and glided over to the back gate. He turned and looked to us.

"What is it, Casey?"

The crow pecked at the gate. I wandered over to look through the wires to the other side, but I saw no friendly chipmunks or any other animals. Then Casey fluttered up to the gate latch and pecked there, scrabbling a little with his feet before dropping back down next to me.

"Do you want us to leave the yard?" Maggie Rose asked.

Casey just stared at her. I headed to the fence and lifted my leg like a male dog, which I do sometimes. I had never seen Casey do that. I couldn't fly like a crow, but I could mark the fence, which was probably more satisfying, anyway.

"Mom," Maggie Rose called. "Is it okay if I leave the yard?"

"Don't go far!" Mom yelled from some-where inside.

When my girl walked over to Casey, he fluttered up over the fence and landed on the other side of the gate. He came to the wires and poked his beak through so that I could sniff him. "Okay," Maggie Rose said, "I have no idea what we're doing, but let's go." Maggie Rose snapped a leash into my collar, and we went for a walk!

It was a very different sort of walk from those I had ever taken before. Casey was mostly on the ground and was hopping and holding his one wing the way he had the very first time I saw him. I remembered that I had followed him when he had been hopping like that, and now we were following him again. Did Casey remember the first day we met? Was that why he was hopping so strangely, so that I would track right behind him?

"Where are you taking us, Casey?" Maggie Rose asked.

I did not know what she was saying, but I thought perhaps she was asking Casey if his wing was hurt again. I hoped not. That would mean Casey had to wear a coat, and with that coat on, he was much less active and never flew anywhere.

Casey led us down the sidewalk, still hopping. Maggie Rose was confused; I could tell by the slow way she was walking.

I passed several yards where dogs had marked, and I wanted to stop and sniff each place, but my girl tugged my leash because Casey didn't know enough to wait for me to paint my own scent over the other dogs'. I liked Casey, but sometimes he could be irritating.

Casey flopped his way over to the base of a tree. Once there, he folded his wings normally. When we came closer, Casey crouched down. Then he started flapping his wings and rose up into the air. He landed in the tree right over our heads, and that is when I smelled it—there was an animal in that tree.

A kitten! Casey had led us to a kitten who was in the tree!

"Oh, my," Maggie Rose said. "There's a little kitten! It's stuck up in the tree! Come on, Lily. We need to go get help!"

Now we were running! I scampered joyously next to my girl. We ran all the way back to Mom's Work, leaving Casey and the kitten back in the tree.

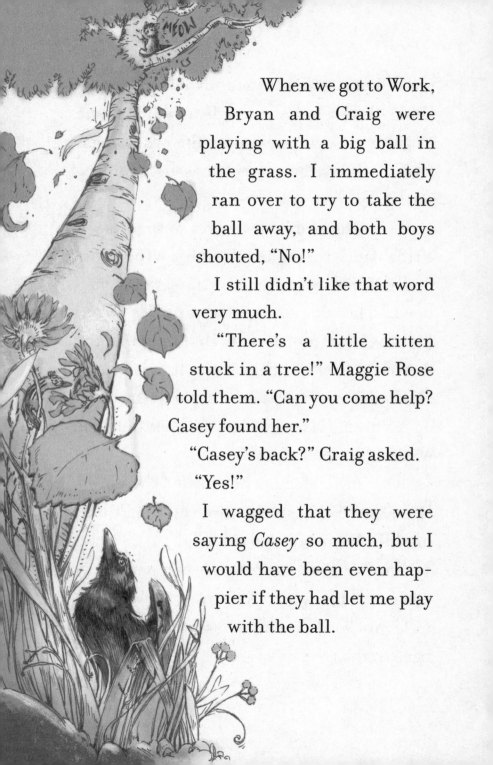

When we got to Work, Bryan and Craig were playing with a big ball in the grass. I immediately ran over to try to take the ball away, and both boys shouted, "No!"

I still didn't like that word very much.

"There's a little kitten stuck in a tree!" Maggie Rose told them. "Can you come help? Casey found her."

"Casey's back?" Craig asked.

"Yes!"

I wagged that they were saying *Casey* so much, but I would have been even happier if they had let me play with the ball.

"Wait a minute," Bryan scoffed. "You mean to tell me the crow led you to a stuck cat? How is that even possible, Runt?"

"Yes, Casey did exactly that, and Dad said to stop calling me *Runt!*"

Craig picked up the ball and tossed it from one hand to the other. I watched, fascinated. "Okay, let's go check it out," he said.

The boys followed us back to the tree where Casey was sitting on a branch near the frightened kitten. Bryan and Craig kicked the ball back and forth all the way, but I didn't try to chase it because I was in no mood to hear them yell, "No!" again.

"Hey!" Bryan said. "The runt was right! There's a kitten stuck in that tree."

We all looked up to where the kitten was still clinging to the trunk of the tree with its little claws. It glanced down at us and opened its mouth and made a very tiny, "Meew."

"I can get it," Craig said. He went to the tree and hugged it. I watched curiously. Then he kicked his legs and hugged the trunk higher, inching his way up the tree.

Maggie Rose clapped her hands together.

I looked at the ball. Maybe I should grab it while Craig was up the tree.

Craig soon made it to the branch where Casey was sitting. He swung himself up, and Casey fluttered his wings a bit, moving over to make room. "The kitten doesn't have a collar," he called down. He reached out his hands, very gently pulling the frightened little kitten off the tree trunk. I could hear the ripping sound her claws made as they were lifted from the bark.

"I have no idea how this little thing got up here," Craig said down to us. "She must have been chased by a dog or something."

I heard the word *dog* and wagged.

Craig put the little kitten inside his shirt and then hugged the tree and slid back down to the ground. He reached up inside his shirt and pulled out the little kitten so that we could all smell it. Well, I smelled it, anyway.

Bryan and Craig and Maggie Rose took the kitten to Mom, who looked it over.

"She's well fed," Mom observed. "She's not a stray. We'll put up notices, and I'm sure her family will come claim her. She must have just escaped from someone's house. Good job saving her, Maggie Rose. And you boys, I'm proud of you."

"Don't forget Casey!" Maggie Rose said. As she spoke, there was a tap. We looked up and saw Casey standing on the window ledge, and he pecked again at the glass. He wanted us to join him in the yard!

Maggie Rose let me out into the yard, and Casey flew up and landed on my back for a dog ride. Mom came out to watch.

"Maybe we could have Lily put on a dog show to raise some money for the shelter." Mom laughed.

I wagged because they were both so happy.

"I could teach Lily tricks!" Maggie Rose said. "Would you like to be in a show, Lily?"

"When I was a little girl, I wanted to put on animal shows on TV," Mom said. "I trained my first dog to jump through hoops and sit on benches and thought someone would drive by and see me and make me a TV star. But what I do now is much better, saving animals every day. You, too, Maggie Rose. I'd rather have you here than on TV. I'd miss you."

"And I would miss Lily. Maybe we should just do our own dog show, here in the yard. Casey can ride Lily's back, and I could teach Brewster to do some tricks, too."

"That could be fun. I'm sure you could teach Casey, too. Did you know that crows are so smart they can learn to say actual words?" Mom asked Maggie Rose.

"What? They can talk?" Maggie Rose said. She sounded delighted.

"Well, they can't have a real conversation, but they can say a few words. When I was growing up, a man down the street had a pet crow who could say, 'I love you.' Only it had trouble with the letter *L,* so it would say, 'I ruv you.' Actually, it was more like, 'I ruv roo.'"

I wagged at Mom's voice, feeling Casey's hard little feet up on my back. Maggie Rose fell to her knees next to me. "Can you talk, Casey?"

I wondered if my girl was asking Casey if he wanted a peanut. Whenever Maggie Rose fed Casey, the crow seemed most excited about the peanuts, even though they were still in the shell.

I might eat a peanut if I had to, but really I'd prefer almost anything else.

"Lily?" Maggie Rose said. "*Lily?* Say *Lily,* Casey? *Lily? Lily?*"

I stared at Maggie Rose, absolutely mystified. What did she want me to do? Why was she saying my name? I looked around the yard, but I could think of no reason why she would be calling to me when I was sitting right here.

"Say *Lily*, Casey! *Lily!*"

Mom chuckled. "Well, I don't know how they learn words, so that might not work, Maggie Rose. But you can keep trying."

"*Lily!* Say *Lily*, Casey?"

Casey and I both stared at my girl. What on earth was she doing?

From that day on, Casey was back to being my friend. He might fly away for a day or longer, but he always came back to see Maggie Rose and me at Work.

That little kitten Casey found didn't live with us very long. In fact, it was the very next day when a woman came. She called the cat *Mittens*, and when Mom took the little cat from her cage to the woman, the woman started crying.

"I was sure I'd lost Mittens," the woman said, wiping her eyes. I could tell her feelings were very strong. Dogs have feelings, too, but mostly they are just happy ones, so we don't ever need to cry. "Thank you so much for saving her!"

"Well," Mom replied, "it was something of a group effort."

When the woman left holding the little kitten, I saw Casey high in the sky. The woman drove away, and Casey followed. I knew that Casey was making sure the kitten was safe.

asey came back that afternoon, and we waited in the yard together for Maggie Rose to quit being at the place called *school* and come play with us. When the gate finally opened and my girl came in, I raced around the yard in a frenzy of joy!

Casey flew right up and landed on my girl's outstretched hand.

"*Lily?* Can you say *Lily*, Casey? *Lily?*"
Maggie Rose asked.

That again. I went to Maggie Rose and
did a very good Sit, thinking if I were the
best dog I could be, we could end this crazy
behavior.

Casey flew over and landed on my head.

I felt him up there, so I held very still. My girl giggled so hard she sat on the ground.

I wagged. Whatever we were doing, it was making Maggie Rose so happy she couldn't even stand up.

"Do you want to go on a picnic, Lily?" Maggie Rose asked.

I had learned that *picnic* meant that we would go to the dog park and sit on a blanket, and Maggie Rose would give me treats out of a basket. I very much liked Doing Picnic.

It turned out that Casey liked picnics, too. He came along to the dog park and flew right down to land on the blanket with us.

Boggs the dog came running over to see us, and Casey wisely flew up in the trees so that Boggs wouldn't sit on him. I was friendly to Boggs, but I watched him closely as he sniffed at the basket with food in it. Those were not his treats in there. I could smell my treats, my girl's snack, and peanuts for Casey.

Maggie Rose called Boggs a good dog, which to me meant she had forgotten about Boggs sitting in the water bowl. Sitting in a water bowl is bad dog behavior and is the sort of thing a dog would never forget.

Boggs ran off to do whatever he was doing, and my girl reached into the basket for the treats. Yes! She had a loop of flashy metal on her wrist. Dangling off this circle of wire were very small dog tags that glittered in the sun.

Casey found the thing fascinating, and he flew down from the tree to sit close to my girl and stare at the dangling dog tags, twisting his head side to side.

"You really like my charm bracelet, don't you, Casey?" Maggie Rose asked him. When Maggie Rose held out her wrist, Casey pecked cautiously at the dangling things.

"Here's a peanut," my girl said. I wagged so that the whole give-a-treat thing would continue—but hopefully with something other than peanuts. Casey took the peanut, which was fine by me.

"*Lily?* Can you say *Lily*, Casey?" Maggie Rose held out a peanut, the dog tags on her wrist glinting. Casey pecked at the flashing metal and took the peanut.

"*Lily?*" Maggie Rose repeated.

I was Lily, and I was right there waiting for my treat. Finally, my girl gave me one. It tasted like dried fish. I wagged, because when Maggie Rose handed me a treat, it meant she loved me. I was her dog, and she was my girl, and Casey was our crow.

As I was eating my treat, Casey flew away to peck at the ground. He came back to our blanket with something in his beak. It was a small glittery object a lot like what was hanging from Maggie Rose's wrist.

"Oh my gosh!" Maggie Rose exclaimed. "You found a charm, Casey! Thank you so much!" Maggie Rose took whatever it was from Casey's beak.

It did not look much like food to me, and so I sat patiently waiting for the topic of treats to come up. My girl fussed with this new shiny thing and then held out her arm—the object Casey had found was now dangling from the loop of flashy wire on her wrist. "Look!" she said.

I wagged, not understanding but happy, anyway.

Maggie Rose reached into the small basket next to her legs and pulled out a peanut. "Here, Casey," she said. "You deserve a reward for bringing me a charm."

Casey took the peanut with his beak and then flew up into the trees to eat it. He dropped the shells, which I found interesting.

The few times I had tried to eat peanuts, I crunched them up, shells and all. Then little bits of what tasted like wood sat on my tongue until I went to the water bowl, sniffed to make sure Boggs hadn't been sitting in it, and then lapped up as much as I could drink. But Casey knew how to open the shells.

A few days later, we did picnic again. This time, I noticed there were several crows in the trees.

None of them came down to see us except Casey, of course. And Casey had something in his mouth. Maggie Rose laughed as she accepted it from him. "Why, Casey, this is so nice of you. It isn't really a charm. It's a dime. But you deserve a reward just the same."

Maggie Rose gave Casey another peanut, and he flew up into the trees. Some of the crows made noises at him. Crows cannot bark. They can only make a loud call that probably is their way of saying they wish they could be dogs.

A little while later, Casey returned with yet another glittery object. Maggie Rose laughed and clapped her hands.

"Casey," she said, "this is wonderful! Let's see what you've got here. Oh! You brought me a tiny bell from a cat collar. This would make a very noisy charm, so I won't wear it, but it's beautiful just the same. Here, Casey." Maggie Rose handed over another peanut from the basket.

Casey looked at me, perhaps to see if I wanted it. But I was waiting for a piece of cheese and had no interest in crow treats.

After cheese, I played Chase-the-Brown-Dog with a dog named Pete, and then several dogs played Chase-Lily-She-Has-the-Ball with me. I drank more water and then plopped down next to my girl, who was eating an apple and holding an object called a *book*.

A book is a dry thing that my girl often stared at as if it were about to come alive and run around. I chewed up a few of them when I was a puppy and found that they tasted even worse than peanut shells.

So now I flopped on my back, my legs in the air, thinking that doing a half Roll Over would earn me another piece of cheese, but Maggie Rose didn't even notice. She never looked up from her book until Casey flew down with something in his mouth, another small, glittery object.

"A bottle cap!" Maggie Rose exclaimed. She gave Casey a peanut. I found the whole process boring, but I stayed on the blanket because I smelled a wonderful slice of meat in a sandwich in the basket.

Then something very alarming happened. When Casey flew up into the tree to drop his peanut shells, another crow landed on our blanket.

Maggie Rose and I held very, very still.

I didn't dare move. I knew that crows who are not Casey are often scared by dogs, and I didn't want to scare this new crow away before I had a chance to make friends with it.

Indeed, this new crow was very nervous. Its legs were bent, and it seemed ready to take flight at the slightest movement.

"Hello there, Mr. Crow," Maggie Rose greeted it very softly.

The crow had something in its mouth. It perched on the edge of the blanket, giving Maggie Rose one of those twisting-head looks that it must have learned from Casey.

"Did you bring that for me?" my girl asked. Maggie Rose very carefully and slowly reached into her basket and brought out one of Casey's peanuts. "That's a metal washer. My dad has some in the garage. I'm sure he'd like another one. Would you like a reward for bringing it to me?" The crow dropped the metal thing from its mouth and bounced forward a few hops and very cautiously removed the peanut from Maggie Rose's fingers.

I followed the crow's flight as it rose up into the trees and realized that all of its crow friends were up there watching this whole thing.

"It's a murder of crows, Lily," Maggie Rose breathed. "And look how many of them are carrying something in their beaks!"

I wagged because she had said my name and because of the smells that came out of that basket when she lifted the lid.

It wasn't long before two more crows had landed on the blanket, each with small, glinting objects in their beaks. Maggie Rose started giggling. "This is so much fun!" she exclaimed.

I was pretty discouraged that picnic had stopped being about pieces of sandwich for a good dog and was now all about the strange crows who kept flying down to land on our blanket, drop metal objects, grab peanuts from Maggie Rose's fingers, and fly away.

This was not how picnic was supposed to be played!

It was, I decided, Casey's fault. None of this would have happened if he hadn't given Maggie Rose a small piece of metal. I never made him try to play one of my games, yet here I was stuck in an endless game of Crows Landing and No Sandwich for Lily.

Soon (much too soon because I had not yet been given a treat), Maggie Rose stood up and folded up the blanket we had been sitting on. "Let's go tell Mom about this!" Maggie Rose said.

Dismally, I followed her out the double gates, sniffing sadly at the basket that was swinging at the end of her arm. My girl had put all the trinkets in that basket. She could have pulled something for a good dog *out* of the basket. But today was all about crows, apparently.

"Look, Mom," Maggie Rose said once we

arrived at Work. "I told you about how Casey was bringing me charms and coins and other little pieces of metal and I was giving him peanuts. Now all the crows are doing it!"

Mom shook her head, using her finger to sort through the worthless trinkets the crows had given Maggie Rose in their effort to ruin the game of picnic.

"Crows are amazingly smart animals," Mom said. "But, Maggie Rose, we can't let them depend on people for their food. We need to untrain this behavior in the crows."

"What do you mean, Mom?"

"Well, like a lot of intelligent animals, crows will do whatever they can not to have to work too hard."

"Like Bryan?" Maggie Rose asked.

Mom laughed. "Maybe. So if you're in the park handing out peanuts, the crows may start thinking that instead of going off to forage for other food, they should just hang out and wait for you to come back. And then what happens when you can't get to the park every day? The crows are thinking, 'Maggie Rose will come back! We don't dare leave the park and miss out on all the free peanuts!' So instead of flying off to find food, they stay there, waiting for you to feed them, getting hungrier and hungrier. At some point, the crows might get so hungry they become sick."

I could see that my girl had lost all of the happiness she had gained at the dog park. I nudged her hand. I knew she'd feel happier if she just remembered to give me a treat.

"I'm sorry, Mom."

"Oh, don't worry, sweetheart. I don't think this has gone on long enough to do any real harm."

The basket was still up there on the table. I wondered if what they were talking about was the best way to give me what was left of Maggie Rose's sandwich.

"What do I do now?" Maggie Rose asked.

"You should take all of these little gifts back to the park and set them on a blanket with you so they can see them. And then don't accept any more trinkets. Even if they drop them right in front of you, don't reward them anymore."

"Not even from Casey?"

"Not even Casey. The other crows will see you feeding him, and they can be pretty stubborn; they'll keep bringing you items until they get another peanut from you. As far as they're concerned, you're feeding all crows, not just your friend Casey."

"Come on, Lily," Maggie Rose said.

We went back to the dog park with the basket and the blanket! It appeared we were going to try picnic again. This time, I sure hoped that Maggie Rose got it right.

12

We sat on the blanket, and Maggie Rose spread out all the items that the crows had brought. I do not know why the crows picked up things like that in the first place. They are not even good to eat.

Immediately, Casey and some of his crow friends landed on the blanket, each with a glittery thing in its beak. I yawned, already bored with the game. I wandered a few steps away and started sniffing at the ground in case anybody had peed there.

I could hear Maggie Rose speaking from behind me. "I'm sorry, birds," she said. "I can't reward you anymore. You can't start to think of me as a way to get food."

The crows hopped around, the trinkets in their beaks. They also looked carefully at all of the glittery items that Maggie Rose had spread out on the blanket, turning their heads one way and another, probably thinking we would all be better off if Maggie Rose would just reach into her basket and give me a piece of her sandwich.

Since there was no sandwich, I picked up a bit of stick and shook it hard. I'm very good at shaking things.

"Do you understand?" Maggie Rose asked. "I brought these back to show I don't want them and won't give you any more peanuts. I'm sorry, but that's what Mom said to do.

Please don't be angry. Please just fly away. Then I'll know you understand. Fly away, crows. Please?"

The crows flapped and hopped and made their dry, croaking noises. I shook the stick even harder, and to my surprise, it flew out of my mouth, heading straight for our blanket.

The stick landed right in the middle of the crows' trinkets. Maggie Rose jumped in surprise, and I raced for the blanket. This was so exciting! It was as if I'd thrown a stick for myself to catch. I bet I was the very first dog who ever managed to do anything like that.

The crows were startled when I leaped onto the blanket and snatched the stick up in my teeth. They flapped up into the air and scattered into the sky. Casey went with them.

I noticed that when the crows landed on the tree branches, they dropped the trinkets from their mouth. The little shiny things fluttered to the ground like peanut shells. The birds all stared down at us with obvious disapproval.

I flopped onto my belly and began to chew my stick into bits.

"Oh, Lily, good," Maggie Rose said softly. "You got them to leave! I think they understand now. They won't be back for more peanuts. Good, Lily. Good dog!"

I was so happy that I was a good dog. I was so happy to feel Maggie Rose's hand on my fur as she stroked my back.

In a minute, I felt something else on my back as well. Casey had landed there. The crows in the trees stared down at us. Probably they had never seen a crow with his own dog before and were wondering how to get one for themselves.

After a while, one by one, the crows flapped away. It was just Casey who was left on the blanket with Maggie Rose and me.

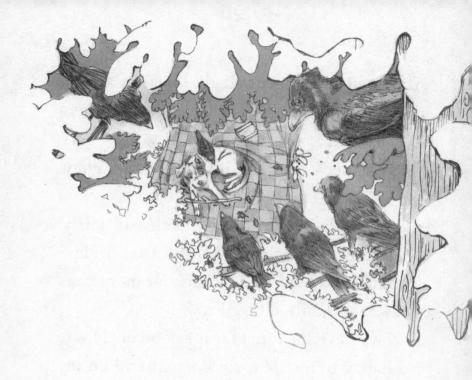

Casey hopped off my back and drew close to Maggie Rose. My girl picked something up off the blanket and held it out to him. "Here, Casey," Maggie Rose said. "I can't give you any more peanuts, but I can give you a charm in case you ever decide to make your own bracelet!"

Casey looked at the thing in Maggie Rose's pinched fingers. Finally, he reached out and snatched it from her hand and flew into the trees.

"Well, Lily," Maggie Rose said to me, "I think they got the message. But it makes me sad. They were just trying to bring me charms, and they probably feel like I didn't like any of their gifts. But I did." She sighed.

"Working in animal rescue is hard, Lily. It seems like it would always be fun, but sometimes you have to clean out the cat cages, and sometimes you have to do something you don't want to do like let an animal go or give a puppy you love to a new family."

Maggie Rose seemed a little sad, so I stopped chewing my stick and nudged her with my nose to let her know that the best way to be happy was to give a dog a bite of some of the sandwich in her basket. I started wagging furiously when she reached inside the basket and pulled out a small bag, which

she opened, letting the marvelous smell of her sandwich into the air.

"Not you, though, Lily. I won't ever have to say good-bye to you."

Just then, Casey fluttered back down and landed on the blanket. I would have to call this bad timing, because Maggie Rose let the hand with the sandwich drop back into the basket. No!

Casey no longer carried the gift that Maggie Rose had given him in his beak. But he had something, and he hopped over to her and offered it.

Maggie Rose laughed happily. "Oh, look, Lily! I gave Casey the charm, and he is rewarding me!"

It was a peanut.

I sighed in disgust.

Maggie Rose took the bag out of the basket, broke off a little piece of sandwich,

Ree-Ree

and gave it to me. At last! Casey watched her feed me.

"Can you say *Lily,* Casey? *Lily?*"

"Ree-ree," Casey croaked. "Ree-ree."

Maggie Rose gasped. "You did it! You said *Lily,* Casey!"

There was so much joy in her voice that I wagged as hard as I could. We were finally Doing Picnic the right way.

MORE ABOUT CROWS

American crows (like Casey) are known as *corvids*. Other corvids include ravens, magpies, and rooks.

Corvids are among the most intelligent birds. Some have been seen using tools. They might poke sticks into trees to search for food or put nuts on roads for cars to crack.

Crows and other corvids can be trained to say words, just as Maggie Rose trains Casey to say, *Lily*.

A female crow lays four or five eggs at a time in a nest that is between one and two feet across.

Crows sometimes bring objects to people, just as Casey and the other crows bring gifts to Maggie Rose. A girl in Seattle began feeding neighborhood crows peanuts and pet food in her backyard, and the crows brought objects back to her—a button, a paper clip, bits of broken glass.

Crows seem to recognize and remember people they don't trust. Some researchers wore masks when they trapped crows to study them. After the crows were released, they made a scolding call to alert other crows to danger if they spotted anyone wearing those masks.

Crows will eat almost anything from seeds, nuts, and fruit to eggs and small animals. They will even grab chicks from other birds' nests to eat.

In the winter, crows sometimes gather together in groups called *roosts.* The largest roosts can have up to two million crows!

Crows sometimes crush the ants and rub them into their feathers. Chemicals in the ants' bodies may keep other insects or parasites away from the crows. It's a bit like spraying themselves with insect repellent.

If a crow dies, other crows may surround it in what is called a *crow funeral,* just as Craig tells Maggie Rose. They seem to be trying to figure out how the crow died.

LILY
TO THE rescue

TWO LITTLE
PIGGIES

For my friends who are working to save them all
at Best Friends Animal Society.

Snow had melted, the birds were in the trees, and I was in the backyard playing ball with my girl, Maggie Rose, her older brother Bryan, and her even older brother Craig.

What a great day! Craig would throw the ball at Bryan, who would try to hit it with a big wooden stick. If he missed, I would run after the ball and grab it and then carry it to

Maggie Rose because I am a good dog who makes sure that everyone gets to play.

When it was Craig's turn to hit the ball, it sometimes went over the fence and into the trees beyond. If that happened, Maggie Rose would open the gate, and I would sniff out where the ball had gone.

The grasses were long and fragrant, full of their own odors, which made it difficult to find the scent of the ball. I had help, though, because there was a crow who was playing with us. His name was Casey, and he was my friend.

I first met Casey at a dog park. He had a wing that did not work well. Then he lived at Work for a little while. (More about Work later.) Now both of his wings are very strong, and he can fly wherever he wants. Some of the time, he wants to fly to where I am for a visit, which I like very much.

Whenever I dashed out of the gate, I looked up into the trees to see where Casey had flown. Usually, Casey chose a branch very close to where the ball lay in the tangle of weeds and shrubs. If I followed Casey, I would get close enough to the ball to catch the scent trail it made as it bounced into the woods. Then, of course, finding it was easy.

I always jumped on the ball and played with it a bit, throwing it up in the air and catching it for myself, because I am a dog who knows how to add extra fun to a game. Then I trotted back to the gate where Maggie

Rose was waiting. I would give her the ball because, as I mentioned, I am a good dog.

Maggie Rose would carry the ball over and hand it to one of her brothers. That disappointed me. When Maggie Rose threw the ball, I could usually catch it on the bounce and then we could really have fun, playing Chase-Me. When Craig or Bryan threw, it was a lot more work to chase the ball down.

"Hey," Craig called to Maggie Rose. "Want a turn at bat?"

I glanced at Maggie Rose curiously. She suddenly seemed a little shy and scared. What had Craig said to her?

"No," she said in a small voice.

"Why not? Come on, give it a try," Craig told her.

Maggie Rose shrugged. "I can't hit it hard. I'm just a runt," she said. Her voice was very quiet.

Craig went up to her with a frown on

his face. He looked at Bryan. "Good going, Bryan," Craig said.

"How is this *my* fault?" Bryan replied.

"You're the one who always calls her a runt," Craig accused.

I went over to Craig, who had the ball. I did Sit so that he would know I was ready to play the game some more. Maybe they had stopped playing because they believed I might not be prepared.

"Well," Bryan replied, "she *is* a runt. She's the shortest girl in the third grade."

Craig frowned at Bryan and then turned back to his sister. "Don't listen to him, Maggie Rose," he said. "You're not a runt." I nosed Maggie Rose's leg because she still seemed a little sad. "Besides, Bryan's the shortest boy in the fifth grade."

"Am not!" Bryan cried.

"Are, too. Come on," Craig said to Maggie Rose. "Take a turn at bat." Craig walked a few steps away from my girl and turned. I sat right next to Maggie Rose. Bryan held out the stick, and Maggie Rose took it from him. She bit her lip and stood with the stick on her shoulder, facing Craig.

Bryan went behind Maggie Rose. "Here," he said. "Choke up on the bat a little." He reached out and moved my girl's hands so that they were higher up on the stick. "That's it."

I wagged because it seemed that something fun was about to happen. I noticed that Casey had soared out of the trees and was watching from his perch on the fence.

"Okay," Craig said to Maggie Rose, "keep your eye on the ball!" Craig gently tossed the ball in our direction. I was about to jump up for it, and it's a good thing I didn't, because Maggie Rose chopped at the air with her stick. The ball bounced into the heavy glove Bryan wore on his hand.

"Strike one!" Bryan called.

"We're not doing strikes right now, Bryan," Craig said.

"No," Maggie Rose said. "He can do strikes." She looked and sounded stubborn. "I want to play with the real rules."

Bryan threw the ball back to Craig. I hoped Craig would drop it and I could chase it. Wasn't that the point of all of this, me chasing the ball?

"Here it comes, Maggie Rose!" Craig called. Maggie Rose tensed. I tensed, too. Craig threw the ball, and it landed on the ground past my girl, and Bryan grabbed it before I could.

This wasn't how we were supposed to be playing the game!

"Strike two!" Maggie Rose called.

"Three strikes and you're out, Maggie Rose," Bryan said as he threw the ball back to Craig.

"Okay," Craig said encouragingly, "third one's a charm!"

Craig carefully moved his hand and the ball sailed through the air and my girl swung her stick and there was a loud thud. She hit it! The ball bounced into the dirt, moving very slowly.

"Run to first base!" Craig called. "Hurry, Maggie Rose!"

Maggie Rose dropped the stick and started to run toward a tree, and I had to make a decision. Bryan was chasing the ball, which

had not gone very far and was already slow-
ing to a stop. On the other hand, my girl was
running, and I loved to run with her.

But I felt that we were still playing ball!
So I dashed past Bryan and leaped on it.

"No!" Bryan bellowed.

No? No what? How did *no* apply to a wonderful situation like this?

"Run to second base!" Craig yelled.

My girl slapped the tree. She switched
direction and started running toward a spot
on the fence behind Craig. Bryan made to

grab the ball from me, and I took off. We were playing Chase-Me! I love this game!

"No, Lily!" Bryan called. "Come here!"

Maggie Rose touched the fence.

"Keep running, Maggie Rose!" Craig cheered. "Go to third, go to third!"

Bryan was still chasing me. Craig can catch me, but Bryan could run all day and all night and he would never be able to get the ball from me. I darted happily around, with Bryan lunging and grabbing and missing.

Maggie Rose jumped on a flat rock with both feet.

"Go home!" Craig shouted happily. He was laughing. "You're going to make it, Maggie Rose!"

Part of what is fun about Chase-Me is letting another dog or a person have the ball sometimes so that the game can reverse and become Chase in the other direction. I bowed with my front legs flat on the ground and my rump high in the air. The ball dropped out of my mouth and bounced between my front paws.

Bryan rushed up and threw himself forward, landing and sliding in the dirt. He picked up the ball!

Bryan ran at Maggie Rose, and I bounded joyfully after him. As he ran, the ball in his hand swung back and forth, and I wanted him to know that I knew we were playing the game of Chase-Bryan-with-the-Ball, so I jumped up to try to grab it from him. Bryan tripped over me and sprawled in the dirt.

"Hurry, Maggie Rose!" Craig called.

Maggie Rose was running as fast as she could, heading back to where she had dropped the stick.

Panting, Bryan stumbled to his feet, his shoes digging into the dirt as he ran at my girl.

"Safe!" Craig yelled. He bounded over and picked up Maggie Rose and swung her around and around, laughing.

Bryan turned and threw the ball with all

his might at the fence. It bounced a few times on the way there, hit the fence, and I caught it in midair!

This game was the best!

The back door of the house slid open, and Mom leaned out. "Maggie Rose? Boys? Would you like to go with me to save some baby pigs?" she called.

C ar ride! Craig sat up in the front next to Mom, and I sat in the back with Maggie Rose and Bryan. They smelled deliciously sweaty in their T-shirts.

"Where are the pigs, Mom? Are we going to a farm?" Craig asked.

Mom shook her head. "No," she replied. "It's the strangest thing. I just got the call. It may even be a hoax. They said there are two baby pigs running around inside a truck stop off the highway. It doesn't seem very likely, but that's what they said."

"What's a hoax?" Maggie Rose asked.

"It's kind of a joke that involves someone telling a lie," Mom replied.

"Well, then," Maggie Rose said, "I hope it's not a hoax because I'd love to see some little piglets. Can I name them, Mom?"

"We'll see," Mom answered.

"If they're boy pigs, then Craig and I should name them," Bryan declared.

"We'll see," Mom repeated.

I wagged because I smelled wonderful things outside the car, things like dogs and trees and horses and other animals. Wherever we were going was probably going to be a lot of fun!

We drove long enough for me to become drowsy in the back seat and fall asleep with my head on Bryan's shoulder. When he said, "Lily, quit breathing on me," I woke up a little and licked his ear. Everyone but Bryan laughed, so I did it again.

Bryan had eaten a peanut butter sandwich earlier, and I could taste it on his ear, which I thought was simply amazing. Why don't all people put peanut butter in their ears? It seemed a very smart thing to do.

I licked Bryan's ear again, and he pushed my face away.

Finally, we arrived at a hot place where the ground was covered with hard cement and the grass and trees were in the distance. Nearby, cars and trucks large and small roared up and down a very busy road.

"Okay, everyone," Mom said. "Stay close to me. I don't know what we're dealing with here."

We walked up to some glass doors, and

when they slid open, a
gust of cold air brought me
delicious food scents: melted cheese; broil-
ing hot dogs; sweet, sticky drinks in cans
and cups.

There was something else as well: two
animals I had never smelled before. There
were animals inside this place!

A large man walked up to greet us. He

smelled a little like meat and a little like plastic. "Are you from the animal rescue?" he asked.

"Yes," Mom replied. "What's this about some pigs?"

The man shrugged. "I was just sitting behind the cash register and the doors opened, and these two pigs came walking in as happy as you please. They're pretty young, these pigs, but they're fast. I tried chasing them—no luck."

The animal smell was coming from something called *pigs*.

"Mom, can I have a candy bar?" Craig asked.

"Me, too!" Bryan said.

"Let's just figure out what we have first, boys. Sir, where are the pigs now?" Mom asked.

"I reckon they're in the back somewhere, probably underneath the sweatshirt rack. That's where I saw them last. I'm a little too old to be chasing critters on my hands and knees."

"All right," Mom said. "Bryan and Craig, you boys start checking up and down the aisles and see if you can spot the pigs. Maggie Rose, you stay with Lily."

I knew the word *Stay* but had never been

fond of it. It meant I should not move until I was told I was a good dog. Sometimes I didn't even get a treat for doing Stay, which was very unfair.

Lily put her hand on my collar and told me to Sit, so I sat. I watched curiously as Mom, Craig, and Bryan crept through this big place.

There was food—I could still smell it—but they didn't seem interested in that. I didn't know why. Instead, they were pushing through big metal racks with pieces of soft cloth hanging from them. They also looked intently at the floor, but there were no treats there.

"I see them!" Craig called.

I watched, completely baffled, as Craig suddenly dropped out of view. A rack of clothing fell over, and I heard a squealing noise. It was an animal sound, and it sounded afraid.

Crash! A shelf with hats collapsed. The big man standing with us groaned quietly.

"They're coming your way, Bryan!" Craig shouted.

I started in amazement when I saw the flash of two pale animals dart across a clear space on the floor. They were both smaller than I was, but very quick. They ran a little bit like dogs, using all four legs. Obviously, these were the pigs!

"I missed!" Bryan yelled. He staggered back, and a cardboard box with bags of nuts hanging from it toppled and fell to the floor. I wagged, thinking that if my friend Casey the crow were here, he would appreciate this. He likes nuts more than just about anything.

All of a sudden, Mom knelt down. Then she stood up, shaking her head. "They just ran right past me, too. They're so fast and wiggly!"

I watched as Bryan and Craig careened

around. Some-
times I caught
a glimpse of the
two pale little
creatures as they
dashed from side to
side. This was fun!
I didn't understand
any of it, but it was
fun!

"All right, boys," Mom
called. "This is obviously
not working. Come on
back."

"Mom," Maggie Rose

said, "maybe we should let Lily see if she can make friends with them."

The boys came slouching up.

"Can I have a candy bar now, Mom?" Craig asked.

"I'll give you both candy bars for free if you'll help put the displays back once we've caught the pigs," the man standing with us said.

Both boys brightened, and I glanced at them curiously. People do things all the time that dogs don't particularly understand, but that doesn't mean it's okay not to pay attention. Right now, Bryan and Craig were alert and happy, though as far as I could see, nothing had changed.

I felt my girl's hand releasing my collar. I shook, yawning, ready for whatever we were going to do next. Now I realized why the boys had suddenly become happy. They knew Maggie Rose was going to let me go!

"Okay, Lily," Maggie Rose said. "Go tell the piggies that they should stop running away."

I heard my name but did not know what my girl was asking me to do. I sat. Doing Sit is one of the first tricks I learned, and it remains one of my most popular.

Then, a movement caught my eye. Underneath a hanging shirt, a pale snout was poking out, sniffing vigorously. I got up and looked at Maggie Rose to see if it was okay for me to stop doing Sit.

She smiled, so I knew that it was. Curious, I trotted down the aisle to take a look. I half expected Maggie Rose to call me back, but she said nothing.

I've learned that some animals are afraid of dogs, even an easygoing dog like me. So, as I got closer to the pig, I began moving more slowly and carefully. I didn't want to startle it.

I saw that my scent had reached that snout because suddenly the nose turned in my direction, twitching and snorting. The little animal poked its face all the way out and stared at me.

My nose and eyes told me several things. First, I had never smelled creatures like this before! They smelled magnificent. A heavy, earthy odor clung to them, along with a mix of other scents that included, oddly, milk.

Second, as the other one poked its head

out at me, I realized they were sisters. There is just something about the common smell of littermates. It doesn't matter if they are dogs or cats or strange four-legged creatures like these pigs. You can always tell.

These two pigs were nearly identical in every way, except that one of them had a small dark patch under one eye. And I could tell they were young. Older and bigger animals are usually slow. These two were twitching and jumping, and their heads and eyes were moving quickly to take everything in. I knew they were babies.

There are some things I understand, and one of them is that for any sort of baby, whether it be a bunny or a kitten or a pig, to be away from its mother is sad. It's not how things should be.

Something bad had happened to these pig sisters.

Or *was* happening.

The two pigs were staring at me, and I was staring at them. I was wagging as I drew near, being very friendly. They were not wagging, but that didn't mean anything. Casey is a very friendly crow, but he has never wagged a tail, not even when Maggie Rose feeds him a peanut.

I decided that they had so much energy I could risk a little movement. I bowed. Then I jumped up, then bowed again.

The two animals understood me! They knew that bowing meant playtime. They surged out from underneath that shirt and leaped on me, squealing and then running around in tight circles. They wanted to play Chase-Me!

I love Chase-Me whether there's a ball involved or not. I decided that the pigs should run after me first. I turned and galloped down in front of some cold glass doors, my feet skittering a little bit on the slick floor.

"Good dog, Lily!" I heard Mom call.

The little creatures came after me. They were fast! I sped up around the corner, looking back over my shoulder. They were both scampering after me at top speed.

I turned another corner, sliding precariously, almost falling, and found myself running right toward Mom and Maggie Rose and her brothers. They were all kneeling. I practically crashed into Craig, my claws

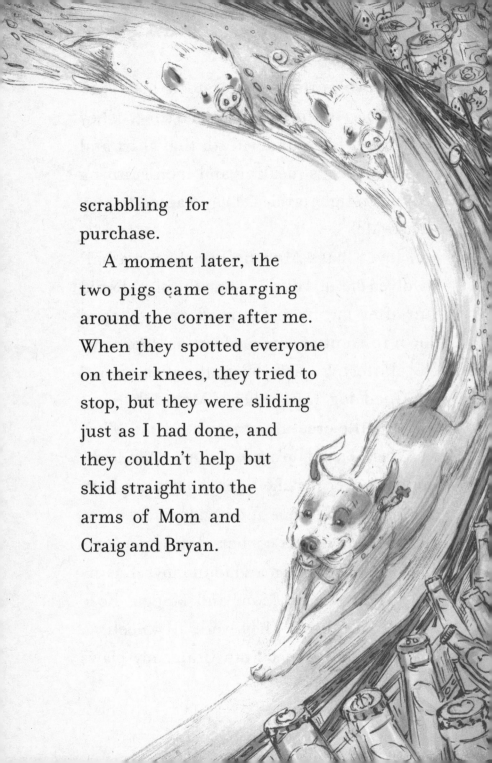

scrabbling for
purchase.

A moment later, the
two pigs came charging
around the corner after me.
When they spotted everyone
on their knees, they tried to
stop, but they were sliding
just as I had done, and
they couldn't help but
skid straight into the
arms of Mom and
Craig and Bryan.

The pigs were not happy and were twisting and squealing, but the boys and Mom had their arms wrapped around them and hugged them tightly.

"Good job!" the man said.

"We'll be right back to help you put your displays up," Craig said.

Maggie Rose grabbed my collar. We all went back out into the sunshine. Mom put the little creatures into a cage in the very back of the truck.

"Good dog," Maggie Rose praised. "You're a good rescue dog today, Lily."

We sat in the truck with the pigs in the back while Craig and Bryan returned to the cool building again and came out a little while later with sweet-smelling candies in their hands. They gave one to Maggie Rose but did not offer any to me because dogs aren't allowed to eat that kind of thing. My girl gave me a chicken treat, which is better, anyway.

On the way home, the little animals were very anxious at first, darting back and forth in their cage. After a while, they collapsed in a heap in the corner of the cage, exhausted.

"How old are the pigs, Mom?" Bryan asked.

"It's hard to say," Mom replied. "But I doubt they can be on their own yet. We'll have to bottle-feed them."

"Do we have pig's milk to feed them?" Craig asked.

"No," Mom admitted, "but we have goat's milk. Goat's milk has a lot of fat in it, and that's what these little girls need right now."

I twisted around to put my paws on the back of the seat, peering into the cage at the two little pigs sleeping in their heap, their small chests rising and falling together. I breathed their scents deeply, drinking them in, learning pig. From now on, this odor would be known to me as the *smell of pigs*.

But there was more to them than that—there was another odor, a complex one, on their skin. I had first noticed this strong smell when I'd followed my family into the cool building.

It was pig, just like the little sisters, but

with a stronger, oily odor, one that was also touched with the faint smell of what was definitely milk. At some time not long ago, these two small pigs had been very close to a bigger, older, milky pig.

The pigs were still asleep when Mom carried their cage into Work. Work is a place with a lot of animals inside it—other dogs, cats, birds, sometimes squirrels. Now Work had two pigs. That was exciting!

I sat in the car with Maggie Rose and the boys, wagging hard and hoping I'd get to go into Work with the pigs and Mom. Lots of times I do get to go there, but not now. Mom came back into the car without the cage or the pigs, and we drove home.

We got out of the car, and I saw Casey sitting on the fence, watching us.

"Ree-ree," Casey croaked. Casey can make noises that sound like talking, and

Ree-ree is often what he says when he sees me, as if he is saying *Lily*. I wagged at him. He probably was wondering when we were going to play ball some more.

I was, too.

We didn't do that, though. The boys rode off on their bicycles, and Maggie Rose sat on the living room floor to play with her Legos. Legos are not very interesting toys because I am not allowed to chew them. That isn't to say I don't try every so often, but it makes my girl sad, so I tried to remember to leave the Legos alone and attack one of my other toys instead.

I decided to see what Mom was doing, so I went to the dining room. She was sitting at the table there, looking at her computer and tapping the keys. People like to do this a lot, even though computers do not smell interesting at all.

I sat under the table. I couldn't smell any

food up there, but I'd had a lot of luck under that table in the past. I lay there patiently but got up when Dad opened the door and walked in. I wagged and pawed his leg, and he petted me.

Getting a full dog greeting is probably one of the things humans like best about walking in the door, so I make sure everyone in the family knows they are loved as soon as they get home.

"What are you looking at?" Dad asked as he gave Mom a kiss.

Mom laughed softly. "I told you about those pigs we just rescued, remember?"

"They're so cute, Dad!" Maggie Rose called out from the living room.

"So I asked the manager who'd called me to send over his surveillance tapes so I could figure out how the pigs wound up inside an interstate truck stop," Mom went on. "Okay, watch this."

Maggie Rose went over to look at Mom's computer, too. She giggled, and Dad laughed, so I wagged.

"The two of them just walked up to the doors like they had an appointment!" Dad marveled. "That's amazing! Where'd they come from?"

"That's the mystery," Mom said. "Watch, here's another angle showing the entire parking lot."

I yawned sleepily, wondering if we'd all play something more exciting soon. I gnawed on Maggie Rose's shoelace, just to pass the time.

"Okay, see," Mom continued. "We've got the parking lot, plus just a little bit of the interstate on the other side. Now watch."

I looked up curiously when Maggie Rose gasped.

"Wait, what just happened?" Dad said.

"First there were no pigs, and then all of a sudden, there they are at the truck stop."

Mom turned and looked at him. "I know. It's as if they appeared by magic. I don't think they crossed that highway, but what else can explain it? And how would they have gotten onto the highway in the first place? I figured they must be from a farm in the area, but I checked and there are no hog farms anywhere nearby, so that's not it. Yet these little girls are *babies*—no way they came from miles away."

"I'm stumped," Dad admitted. "I don't know what to think."

"Well, either way, they're here now. Those piglets are going to wake up very hungry. I've already told our supplier that we need a *lot* of goat milk."

"You're telling me they eat like pigs," Dad said with a chuckle. I wagged at the laughter.

"I'm telling you every two hours, twenty-four hours a day, for at least the next several days," Mom replied.

"Every *two hours*? All night long? Are you serious?"

"Welcome to animal rescue," she said.

"I'll help!" Maggie Rose said eagerly.

Mom smiled. "I know you will, sweetie. But we're going to need the whole family to make this work."

"Huh. Actually," Dad replied, "I was thinking of driving up to Evergreen to see if I can spot that black bear people have been talking about."

"Oh, *really*?" Mom said. "You're going to do that and also help feed the pigs?"

"Um," Dad answered slowly. "I sort of thought if I wasn't here, you'd be the one to feed them all night."

"Do you remember, James," Mom responded lightly, "when I had to get up in the middle of the night to be with our newborn babies? You said you couldn't do it because it was the 'mom's job.'"

"Why do I get the feeling you're never going to let me forget that?" Dad replied.

Maggie Rose giggled.

Mom reached into a bag on the table next to her and pulled out two glass bottles. "Well," she said cheerfully, "I've decided that feeding pigs is a dad's job."

Dad picked up one of the glass bottles and held it with a funny look on his face while Maggie Rose laughed so hard she fell down, and I got to jump on her and lick her face and chew on her hair. At last, we were playing something fun!

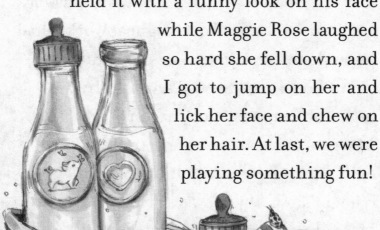

4

That night was the best! Dad and Maggie Rose and I stayed overnight at Work. I had never done that before. I was so excited!

At Work, most of the animals live in cages or kennels. I'm the only one who gets to be out, roaming around, sniffing and greeting all my old friends and any new arrivals. Most of the animals don't stay at Work too long—they leave after a few days or weeks, usually when a happy person or a family full of happy people comes to get them.

I'm sad to see my friends leave Work, but they and the people are so happy it makes up for it. Plus, there are always new friends to get to know.

That night, Brewster, the old dog who mostly takes naps, came out to sleep with me on a blanket.

Maggie Rose stretched out on a mat on the floor, while Dad lay down on the narrow bed

where Maggie Rose sometimes lies down to read her books when she comes to Work.

The pigs, however, hardly slept at all. They squealed and snorted, and when Dad picked up one of them and pushed a bottle into her mouth, the delicious aroma of warm milk filled the air. Brewster and I would look at each other with bewildered expressions. Why did pigs get milk while there was none for dogs? What was going on here?

While one pig was being fed, the other one raced around on the floor, diving under Dad's bed, leaping up on top of me and

Brewster, making Maggie Rose laugh, and just generally going completely pig.

They were fantastic playmates. They loved to play Chase-Me, whether they were tearing after me or each other or running away from me when it was my turn to chase.

Dad would lie back on his bed, and the pigs would dart over to him and squeal to make sure he was paying attention to them. They were locked out of the big room where most of the animals slept in their cages, so they ran around and around the room where we were playing and tipped over a small table and bashed into a shelf and crashed into some chairs.

Brewster slept through most of this and was very grumpy when one of the pigs jumped on him. This happened many times. Brewster kept staring at me as if he thought I should do something to make the pigs behave.

Why would I, when we were all having so much fun?

Dad never took a bottle and gave me milk, but he sure enjoyed doing that with the pigs. Maggie Rose did it, too. After a while, though, she lay down on her mat and closed her eyes and stayed there, and Dad fed both of the pigs.

Again and again, I'd look over to see him holding one or the other in his lap, feeding them, his eyes half-closed.

"I can't believe I have to do this again so soon, Lily," Dad said with a sigh. I wondered if he was telling me how much fun we were having at Work all night long. "How can they eat so much?"

I heard the question and did Sit. What else could I do under the circumstances?

At one point, the two wiggly pigs curled up against Brewster's warm side.

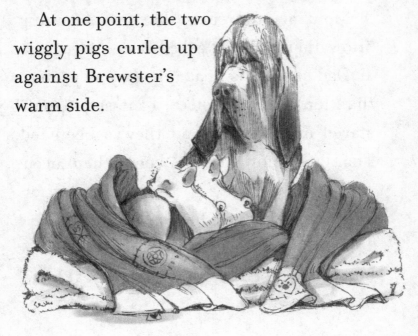

I lay down with Maggie Rose, and Dad flopped back on his bed, and I thought we were all going to sleep for a good long time.

I was wrong, though, because pretty soon, the pigs started squealing again. Maggie Rose didn't stir, but Brewster picked up his head and snorted, and Dad had both hands over his eyes. "No. No, please," he begged.

I wagged. Dad fed the pigs some more. It seemed to be his new favorite thing to do.

Mom arrived early the next morning. "How did it go?" she asked Dad.

Dad shook his head. "If they slept more than ten minutes apiece, I missed it, but I stayed on schedule and they've been fed. Thank God for Lily. She keeps them occupied."

I wagged because he'd said my name.

"I'll take over feeding them. Will you go home and get the kids some breakfast?" Mom asked.

"Sure," Dad agreed. "And then I'm going to bed. Today, Dad's job is to take a nap."

I woke up Maggie Rose by licking her ears, and we left Work and went home. The rest of my family was seated at the table. Craig fed me some eggs, and Maggie Rose told me I was a good dog.

After we ate, Craig and Bryan went

outside, Maggie Rose lay down with a book, and Dad did something very curious—he climbed into his bed. I had never seen him go back to bed in the middle of the day before!

I was tired from chasing pigs all night and wondered if he would let me climb up to be with him.

He did.

Everything was different now that I had two pig friends at Work. Maggie Rose gave them names; the fast one was called Scamper, and the really fast one was called Dash. Scamper and Dash spent all of their time either lying in people's laps being given milk from bottles, skittering around Work like crazy playing Chase-Me, getting me to play Chase-Me-I'm-a-Pig, or sleeping.

They went into their naps like they did everything else: with a crash. One moment they would be careening around, sliding and squealing, and the next they would be collapsed in a pile of pig, eyes shut, noses twitching.

When I wanted to nap, I usually went to find Brewster. I like the way Brewster settles down for a doze. He paws at his bed, getting it properly rumpled up, turns around a few times, and then lies heavily down.

And when he wakes up, he does it properly, yawning and stretching and scratching himself and then lying around getting used to the idea of being awake. The pigs, on the other hand, woke up on the run. They would be completely still one moment and doing Chase-Me an instant later.

I got to go to Work most nights, which was amazing! Sometimes I'd be there with Mom, sometimes with Dad. Every now and then, Bryan or Craig or Maggie Rose would come, too. I loved that!

The people didn't seem as happy as I was, though.

"When is this going to end?" Craig groaned at one point.

"I'm tired," Bryan agreed, holding Dash in his lap. "This is boring."

"I'll do it," Maggie Rose said. Bryan gave Dash to her.

"Animal rescue isn't always about cuddling puppies and kittens," Mom told us. "It's hard work. But think what we've done. These little girl piggies wouldn't survive if it weren't for us."

"And Lily!" my girl chimed.

"And Lily," Mom agreed.

I wagged, though no treats resulted from all this talk about me.

Now, I loved my new pig friends. They were fun to play with. But I did not see why no one thought that a good dog should be given milk from a bottle, since that was what we were doing with Scamper and Dash.

Brewster wasn't fed any milk, either, but

he didn't seem to care about that. What he did care about was how the pigs would run over and jump on him. He did not seem to like it. He didn't growl, but he did groan a lot. I tried to herd the pigs away from Brewster when I could.

"This is killing me," Dad complained one day.

We had been at Work all day. Now Brewster was deep into a nap, and I was watching jealously as Mom and Dad sat in chairs and gave the little pigs a meal.

"It's killing us," Mom corrected tiredly. "They have so much energy!"

"I think we need to get these little girls feeding on their own," Dad said. "I can't do this much longer, and you've got other animals to take care of at the rescue."

"You're right," Mom replied resignedly. "They're for sure old enough to feed themselves, but I don't know what to do. I put goat

milk in a bowl, but they weren't at all interested. I think they prefer being bottle-fed. It
makes them feel loved."

Mom's phone jangled in her pocket, and
she reached in awkwardly and held it up to
her ear. "Hello?" she said sleepily.

Then she sat bolt upright and didn't seem
to notice as the bottle slipped out of Dash's
mouth.

"Oh no," she said. "Oh, goodness! I'll be
right there." She got up and dumped Dash in
Dad's lap.

"What happened?" Dad asked. He looked
worried. I sat up, watching both of their faces
intently in case they needed my help.

"That was the school," Mom said. "Maggie
Rose fell asleep in class, and she slid right
out of her chair onto the floor."

I heard my girl's name and gazed around
alertly for her, but I didn't see or smell her
anywhere near.

Dad and Mom looked at each other.

"You'd better go get her," Dad said with a sigh. He looked down at the pigs in his lap. "When you're back, we'll figure out something to do."

5

Mom left, and Dad finished feeding Scamper and Dash. We all played Chase-Me until Mom came back again. She had my girl with her! Maggie Rose!

I ran to my girl and greeted her with my tail wiggling back and forth. I licked her knees and her hands when she reached down to scratch me.

Mom and Dad seemed to think that Maggie Rose needed a lot of attention, too. They fussed over her until they got her settled on the long, narrow bed where Dad sometimes lay down when we were doing Work at night, feeding the pigs and playing Chase-Me.

"But I'm not sick or anything!" Maggie Rose said. "I just got sleepy."

"Lie right there and close your eyes," Mom said. "You're going to take a nice long nap. And no more overnights at the rescue for you. That's final."

"But who's going to help feed the pigs?" Maggie Rose asked. She sounded worried. I jumped up onto the skinny bed with her and snuggled up against her so she'd know I'd always take care of her.

Mom sighed. "We'll figure it out. Right now, rest."

"Can I have my snack from school first?" Maggie Rose asked. "I'm hungry."

Maggie Rose had put down her backpack next to the bed. Mom unzipped it and reached in and pulled out a crinkly bag and handed it to Maggie Rose.

I sat up with my ears perked high. Crinkly bags are excellent for having treats in them!

Sure enough, Maggie Rose began taking things out of the bag and putting them in her mouth. I sniffed but could not smell anything particularly delicious.

"Want a blueberry, Lily?" Maggie Rose asked me. She held out her hand. There was a small dark fruit in her palm, but it did not interest me.

The two pigs ran over to see what we were doing. They couldn't jump up on the couch like me, but they stretched their necks as high as they could. Their little snouts were twitching like mad. "Hey, Mom," Maggie Rose asked, "can I feed Scamper and Dash some blueberries?"

Mom and Dad glanced at each other. "Sure, why not?" Mom agreed.

My girl held out fruits in each hand, one for Scamper, and one for Dash. The pigs shoved their mouths right into her open palms and scarfed them up. Maggie Rose laughed. "They love blueberries!" she sang.

Mom stood and walked over. Scamper and Dash were not doing Sit because they were pigs and not dogs, but they were trying to do something like it with their eyes, staring up at my girl eagerly.

"Do you think I could have some of those blueberries?" Mom asked.

Maggie Rose handed over the crinkly bag that had been so disappointing to me. Mom went to the refrigerator and pulled out a bottle. The refrigerator at home has wonderful smells that charge out into the room every time the door is open, but the one here at Work is much less interesting.

I perked up when I caught the scent of what Mom was pouring into the bowl on the counter. It was some of that rich, fragrant milk that the pigs were always eating. Food in a bottle might be for Scamper and Dash, but food in a bowl was for a good dog!

Scamper and Dash must have known this because they turned and headed out the door and down the hall, probably to jump on Brewster or knock over some furniture.

I was disappointed to see Mom toss some of Maggie Rose's fruits into my bowl of milk. I decided, though, that I could lap up the milk and leave the little fruits. This is just one of the things dogs must learn to do.

"Maggie Rose," Mom said. "Can you hold on to Lily for just a moment?"

I heard my name and figured that Mom was telling my girl that I was finally about to be fed some of the delicious milk. Then Maggie Rose wrapped her arms around me, holding me on her lap. That was a strange thing to do, because now I couldn't get at the bowlful of milk!

"Good dog," my girl said to me.

Good dog? *Good dog?* What happened next was not the sort of thing that should happen to a good dog!

"Okay!" Mom said. "Scamper! Dash! Come have some breakfast."

My new pig friends had learned their names a little bit and came racing into the room, either because Mom had called them or because they just felt like it.

That's how they did things. They were not like dogs, who must pay attention to what people want. They were just crazy pigs, who thought their job should be to run around and then have milk even though a good dog doesn't get any.

Mom put the big bowl down on the floor, and I naturally surged forward, but my girl's hands held me still. What were we doing?

Scamper and Dash shoved their noses

into my dog bowl. Milk went flying every-where, and my pig friends started to eat my treat! What were they doing?

"The blueberries worked!" Mom exclaimed.

Dad was smiling. "This could change our lives forever," he said with a laugh. "No more bottle-feeding around the clock!"

I did not understand why Mom and Dad seemed so happy when right in front of their eyes these pigs were taking my treat.

"They love blueberries," Maggie Rose said with a cheerful grin.

I looked at her in dismay. She did not seem at all unhappy that these pigs were busily making sure that I would not get any milk from my bowl.

Soon, Scamper and Dash were done ruining my morning and took off running again. Maggie Rose released me, and I went over and sniffed the bowl, licking up a few drops of milk that were splattered on the floor. It was as delicious as I had supposed.

I mournfully examined the now clean bowl, smelling the remnants of some of Maggie Rose's fruits as well the faintest hint of my milk, all gone to the pigs.

That night at dinner, I sprawled forlornly under the table, thinking about how wonderful it would have been to have my milk. Mom said both pigs' names, and I figured that was what the family was discussing: how Scamper and Dash had gobbled up my food by mistake while Maggie Rose forgot to let go of me.

"I have that appointment up in the foothills tomorrow," Dad said. "I'll take Maggie Rose and Lily with me." I raised my head at my name but otherwise didn't react. There really was nothing surprising to me about the fact that everyone was sitting at the dinner table discussing what a good dog I am.

"From what you said about the ranch, it seems promising," Mom replied.

"Can I go?" Bryan asked.

"You boys both have soccer," Mom replied.

"Is it a pig ranch?" Maggie Rose asked.

"No," Dad said. "But it might work out for Scamper and Dash. The rancher wants their manure for his compost. Up in the hills, it's tough to get a good compost heap going because it's so dry. If they try to add food scraps, it'll just attract raccoons or other scavengers."

"What's compost?" Maggie Rose asked.

"Oh, it's stuff like dead leaves or grass clippings and leftover food and animal manure, too," Dad replied. "It'll become natural fertilizer if you let it rot in just the right way. So Scamper and Dash can help with that.

"He says he's got an electrified, fenced-in pen that he can move each day for them. They'll do what pigs do, which is to churn the soil underneath their feet. Pigs love to wallow in mud. So it'll be good for everyone— at least, that's what he claims. We'll have to see."

6

The next day, we took
Scamper and Dash
for a car ride!

Dad drove. Maggie Rose and I sat in the
back seat, where I could keep an eye on the
pigs who were in their cage in the far back.
They made a lot of squealing noises when we
first started driving, but then they settled
down for a nap.

They liked to sleep on top of each other,
and I noticed that when Scamper twitched

her ears, Dash twitched her ears at exactly the same time. This is not something dogs do. If I move my ears, Brewster doesn't move his.

Was this why the pigs were given milk and I wasn't? Did my human family think that twitching ears deserved a treat, just like Maggie Rose gives me a treat for doing Roll Over?

It is hard to tell what people are thinking sometimes. Ear twitching didn't seem like much of a trick, but then again, neither did Roll Over, when I thought about it.

We drove for some time, and I figured we were headed back to where I'd first met my little pig friends, a place with food smells and clothing hanging down for Bryan and Craig to push over. Instead, we wound up at a spot that smelled powerfully of cows and horses.

We parked in the shade of a large tree, and Maggie Rose and Dad and I jumped out. Scamper and Dash had woken up, but they stayed where they were, lifting their noses inside their cage.

A man in dusty clothing came over and held out his hand. "It's nice to meet you, Mr. Cleveland," Dad told him. "I'm James Murphy. This is my daughter, Maggie Rose."

"Call me Owen," the man replied.

My nose was up and twitching like mad. I could smell animals, but I could not see any.

"I'm sure glad you're here," the man in dusty pants said. "My boy found an abandoned fawn, and we were thinking we needed to call somebody, and then I remembered that I was getting a visit from a game warden today." I felt Dad stiffen, and Maggie Rose and I both glanced at him curiously.

"Did you touch it?" Dad asked.

Dirty Pants Man shook his head. "Nope, but she's clearly starving."

"I need to see it right now," Dad said. "Can you take me to it?"

Maggie Rose put my leash on my collar. Dad opened the back of our truck, lifted out the cage, and set Scamper and Dash on the ground in the shade. They charged up to the door and looked like they were waiting to get out and run around.

Dad, however, did not let them out. This

was a time for dogs, not pigs, to walk with people.

We followed the man across some ground toward a stand of lush trees. His clothing gave off clouds of dust as he walked.

That's when I saw the horses standing at a fence and staring at us. They seemed surprised that there could be anything so wonderful as a dog visiting their home. I wanted to trot over and sniff them and say hello, but my job was to be with my girl, and she was with Dad.

"What do we do, Dad?" Maggie Rose asked. "If the deer is starving?"

Dad rubbed his jaw. "Well, a doe will leave a newborn fawn alone by itself for as much as twelve hours at a time. I suspect that we're not dealing with a starving animal, probably just a newborn who hasn't yet fed enough to get any meat on her bones."

I think I was probably the first one to

smell it: a new creature, female, young, furry but not a dog. I had met an animal who smelled like this once before, something with long legs that Dad had called a *deer*.

The man with the dirty pants slowed, crouched, and pointed. I guessed that he could smell the deer, too. "See? Right there, under that tree."

I could see the thing now. It was small, a little smaller than I am. It had big dark eyes and ears that stuck out from its head. It wasn't moving at all—like a dog who has been told to do Stay.

Painted over this foreign creature's scent was another smell, the same sort of animal, but different—bigger, older. Also, I could detect an odd, faint, milky odor as well.

It reminded me of when Scamper and Dash would climb on top of Brewster and irritate him out of his nap. After they had roused him, the pigs would smell a tiny bit like Brewster, and he would smell a tiny bit like them. That's what I supposed might have happened here. This small deer had been napping with another, older one.

That did not explain the milk, though. Perhaps earlier, Dirty Pants Man had been here with a bottle of milk. It was discouraging to think that all these animals were being given milk but a dog wasn't.

See?" Dirty Pants Man whispered. "The poor thing is like to starving."

"No," Dad replied. "It's what I'd thought:

this fawn was just born yesterday. Its mother left it here to go forage. In fact, I wouldn't be surprised if she's very close by, watching us."

As we were sitting there, I picked up a new hint of the odor that was on the little deer. The animal that had been lying with it was somewhere over in a deeper stand of trees. I looked and could not see it, but I sure could smell it! The milk odor was also stronger, too, now that I knew to sniff for it.

"So the baby deer is okay, Dad?" Maggie Rose asked.

"Yes," Dad replied. "All we need to do is leave it alone. Its mother will take care of the rest."

Dad straightened up, and that's when I caught the faintest movement. There it was—a bigger deer, just like the small one except for its size. It was staring at us with-out moving a muscle. Maybe it was like

Brewster and didn't like to move any more than it had to.

Dirty Pants Man smiled. "Well, you learn something new every day," he said. "I for sure thought I needed to help it."

"Don't worry, this happens all the time," Dad replied. "People mean well, and when they see a newborn fawn, they think it must be abandoned because they're so skinny and aren't moving, as if they're too weak to stand up. But that's their instinct. The fawn couldn't possibly run away from predators, so all it can do is lie still and hope nothing spots it. Often, people bring a baby deer to us at the wildlife refuge, but it's very hard to raise them by hand. It's almost always best to leave them where they are."

We were done looking at the little creature and smelling the other one in the woods, because we turned away and headed back. The man with the dusty pants walked with us to our truck.

"So, don't you think this would be a good place for your rescue piglets?" the man asked.

"Well, that depends," Dad replied.

I did Sit because apparently Dad and Dirty Pants Man were planning to talk for a while.

"See," Dad explained, "I didn't realize you were so close to the foothills. Probably a lot of predators up there that might come down if they pick up the scent of pigs. Does your portable cage have a lid on it?"

"A lid?" the man replied slowly. "Nope,

didn't think I'd need one. They aren't *flying* pigs, are they?"

The men laughed.

Maggie Rose spoke up. "The lid is to keep out animals that can climb, like mountain lions. And eagles, even, if the pigs are little."

"That's my game warden girl," Dad said with a smile. "She's absolutely right."

The man shook his head. "Too bad. Well, I hope you find these little ladies a good home."

Dad picked up the cage with the little pigs in it and put it in the truck. Maggie Rose and I and Dad got in, but the man with the dirty pants did not, so he probably didn't want to take a car ride with a couple of pigs in the back.

"Well, I do appreciate you setting me straight about that little fawn. I thought it was starving for sure," he told us.

"You're welcome," Dad replied.

Dad started the truck, and with a wave from my girl, we all drove away.

"You were absolutely right about the cage, Maggie Rose," Dad said. "I bet Mr. Cleveland doesn't think about predators because he mostly has horses and cows. Mountain lions won't attack a herd of big animals unless they're desperate, and both horses and cows can protect their young. But Scamper and Dash are almost defenseless."

"We can't let anything happen to the pigs," Maggie Rose declared firmly.

"I know, Maggie Rose. There's another rancher who responded to our posting," Dad said. "We're headed there now. Maybe he'll have a better situation."

I grew sleepy as we drove, but I was unable to nap because Scamper and Dash kept squealing and jumping around in their cage.

We stopped again at a new place and got

out. It smelled a lot like where we had just been. There was the distinct odor of horses on the air, and I saw a few of them walking in the grass.

Horses do not know how to play fun games the way dogs do. I have never seen one chase a ball or wrestle with others in the park. All they do is stand around and look at one another or at the grass they are chewing on. One dog is more fun than all the horses I've ever seen in my life put together.

A man came out of his house as Dad lifted out the cage with the pigs in it and put it on the ground again. Next to the man, there was a boy who looked like he was Maggie Rose's age.

The boy ran up to us and then stopped. "Hi."

Maggie Rose looked at the ground for a moment, maybe trying to figure out what it was that horses found so fascinating about grass. "Hi," she said.

"My name's Bobby," the boy told her.

"I'm Maggie Rose," my girl said.

"Huh," the boy replied. "Is Rose your last name, or is that your middle name?"

"My middle name. I'm Maggie Rose Murphy," Maggie Rose said.

"Well, I'm Bobby Jacob Dell," the boy replied.

I could see this was going to be one of those times when people stood around talking for a long while. When that happens, all a good dog can do is either wait for them to play or go off on her own. Since I was off leash, I had wandered away, sniffing at the bases of trees and along the tires of our truck, when I saw something overhead. It was Casey the crow, my best friend!

Casey likes to follow me around and land

on my back. Lately, he had started chasing us when we did Car Ride in the truck.

He turned lazy circles overhead before fluttering down on a tree branch just above the cage where Scamper and Dash were busily wrestling with each other.

And that's when I smelled it: a very familiar scent was coming to me on the breeze.

Frankly, it smelled a lot like Scamper and Dash, so I knew instantly that it was pig. In that moment, I recalled the big animal watching us as the baby animal lay on the ground. There had been a milk smell on the large creature, and I now understood that it was the mother of the little animal in the grass.

That's why the two animals' scents had been mingled. The mother had been lying with the little animal. Mothers do that sort of thing. My mother used to, in the time when I lived with her and not with Maggie Rose.

This made me remember something else. When I first met Scamper and Dash, they had been coated with a thick blanket of odor. It had smelled like grown-up pig and also a little bit like milk.

Obviously, what I had smelled on Scamper and Dash was a mother smell. Scamper and Dash had a mother! And the familiar odor coming to me now was that very same pig.

I do not know if the two little pigs smelled their mother, but I sure did. I went to the cage, and we touched noses. Scamper and Dash were, as usual, full of energy and wanting to race around even inside the small cage. If I were in there, we would all be wrestling.

I knew if I wanted to be a really good friend to them, I would lead them toward that mother scent.

When animals are very young, they need to be with their mothers. I used to be with mine. Even though I had to share her with too many brothers, I loved being near her.

I didn't need my mother anymore, because I had Maggie Rose now. But the little pigs were different. They were younger than I was. And they didn't have their own people yet, the way I had my girl.

If the little pigs were going to reach their mother, they needed to come out of the cage.

I pawed at the cage door, frustrated that it was locked. I looked over at my girl to see if she was willing to come help me. However, she was busy talking to the boy her age while Dad was busy talking to the man his age. I would have to help my friends on my own.

I pawed at the door again, and the pigs watched curiously. They did not know what I was doing, but they were very interested in it, anyway.

With a flutter, Casey the crow landed on the bars at the top of the cage. This was very exciting to the two pigs, who raced around in small circles and then jumped on each other.

Casey was watching me, though, not the pigs. He twisted his head one way and the other, in a gesture that I had learned meant that he was trying to figure something out.

I raised my paw to the cage door again. The crow spread his wings and lifted himself off the top of the cage and landed right on my head!

I sat and held still, because Casey doesn't like it when I run around with him up there. The two pigs looked absolutely dumbfounded to see a bird on a dog's head. I waited patiently to see what Casey would do next.

Casey fluttered up off me and pecked at the cage door, gripping the wires with his feet so that he hung there, going *peck, peck, peck.* I watched as he did this for what seemed a long time. Then suddenly, with a rattle, the cage door opened!

Instantly, Scamper and Dash charged out, so thrilled to be free that they were paying absolutely no attention to where they were running. I watched as they vanished around the corner of the house, and then I took off in pursuit.

Scamper and Dash are very fast, but I was able to catch up with them. As soon as I did, their game shifted from Let's-Chase-Small-Pigs to Let's-Chase-Lily!

I could smell the scent of the mother pig as clearly as anything I had ever smelled. Since the two little pigs were already chasing me, I turned and ran straight for some trees, tracking the scent as if it were a trail in the dirt. Scamper and Dash instantly followed.

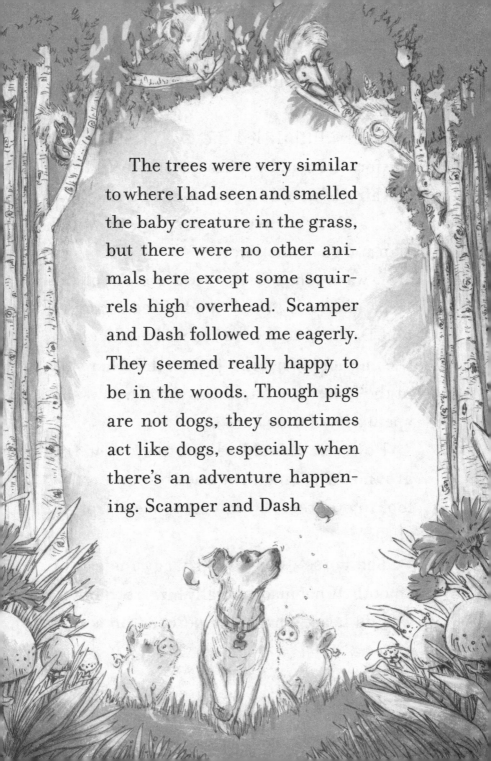

The trees were very similar to where I had seen and smelled the baby creature in the grass, but there were no other animals here except some squirrels high overhead. Scamper and Dash followed me eagerly. They seemed really happy to be in the woods. Though pigs are not dogs, they sometimes act like dogs, especially when there's an adventure happening. Scamper and Dash were as excited to race through the woods as I was.

As I skillfully led the two pigs through the forest, I could see Casey tracking us from the air. He would flutter along and land in a tree, and then when we passed it, he would flap and go to another tree.

It wasn't long before we were out of the trees and in a grassy field. I led Scamper and Dash up to a wire fence. I could smell the mother pig nearby, just on the other side of the fence. Her smell was strong, as if she spent a lot of time here.

However, I could see no pigs, just flat ground. After a moment, one of the strangest-looking horses I had ever seen trotted closer.

The horse's body was shaggy instead of smooth. What made it really bizarre, though, was its head, which was perched on a very long neck. Most horses have ridiculously large heads, with huge noses. This horse-thing had a face more like a dog's and ears that stuck straight up.

The horse creature spotted me and came directly over to where Scamper, Dash, and I were huddled near the fence. I did not know if I should bark or not. The horse-thing was odd, but it didn't seem to be a threat. In fact, it seemed more curious than anything, gawking at me.

It was probably astounded to see an amazing dog and her pig friends.

After a time of staring at the horse creature and having it stare back, I heard a woman's voice. "What do you see?" the woman called.

I wagged as I saw a woman walking slowly across the field toward us. The odd horse turned its head to look at her.

"What is it?" the woman asked.

I decided that this horse creature couldn't talk any better than regular horses, or it would have responded by now.

All of a sudden, the woman clapped her

hands together. "Piggies!" she said, and she started moving very swiftly toward us. "Piggies!"

She was obviously happy to see me, which made sense, because I am a dog.

When she was very close, she turned to look back and put her fingers to her lips. There was a very loud, very shrill whistle. "Pigpig-pig-pig!" she called in a high voice.

I wondered if she had a dog named Pigpig-pig-pig.

But instead of a dog, a big, fat, pale-colored pig appeared around a corner of a house on the other side of the field. She came waddling toward us, and I knew at once that she was the pig I had been smelling since we had arrived! There was no longer a milk scent clinging to her, but she was definitely the source of the odor that had been painted all over Scamper and Dash the day I'd first met them.

My little pig friends began squealing. At the sound of their voices, the mother's trot broke into a full-out gallop—not a fast gallop, though. When animals get older, they don't move as quickly as Scamper and Dash. But I could tell that she was moving as swiftly as she could manage.

She raced toward us while the horse creature stood frozen, clearly not sure what was going on.

I honestly didn't understand everything myself. But the woman was now very close, and I knew that she would take charge the way people always do.

"Could it be?" the woman asked. I heard the question in her voice and wagged, thinking she was asking me if I was a good dog. Obviously, I was.

The woman was now right up to the fence, and the horse creature took a step back from

her. She reached a hand through the wires, and I licked it.

Then the mother pig arrived. My little pig friends went completely crazy, squealing and squawking and rubbing up against the wires and pressing their snouts at their mother.

Their mother was squealing, too. "Come on, pig," the woman urged. She began walking along the inside of the fence, and so I led Scamper and Dash in the same direction. Casey was watching from a nearby tree.

The horse creature decided to tag along with us because I was a dog and obviously knew what to do when things are confusing. There was a good long stretch of fence, but after a while, the woman came to a gate.

She pushed it open. My two pig friends burst past me and ran to their mother, so I followed.

The woman shut me into her yard with a clank of the gate.

"I don't understand how this happened," the woman marveled. "But these are your babies, aren't they, Sadie?" she asked the big pig.

Scamper and Dash were leaping all over their mother as if she were Brewster trying to take a nap. She was nuzzling them and making low, happy cries.

Just then, I heard a high voice coming from the direction of the trees. "Lily!" the voice called.

It was Maggie Rose.

9

Well, even though my girl was yelling for me, I couldn't run to her because I was in a yard behind a fence! When I heard Dad call my name, I barked. The moment I barked, that horse creature regarded me in absolute amazement.

A lot of animals are really impressed when they hear a dog barking, as well they should be.

I went to the gate and did Sit, being a good

dog, expecting the woman to open it, but she did not. I looked up in the air to see if Casey could fly down to help. He'd opened the pigs' cage, so he could probably open this gate, too.

But Casey was still in the trees and didn't seem to know I needed his aid.

Every time I heard Maggie Rose's voice calling my name, it sounded closer, and I joyously barked right back. Soon, I saw Dad and Maggie Rose emerge from the trees, their scents coming to me on the air.

"Lily!" Maggie Rose called again. She broke from Dad's side and ran up to the fence, so I was able to push my nose through the wire to touch her outstretched hand. "What are you doing here, Lily?" Maggie Rose asked.

Dad approached, peering at the big pig and the woman. He took off his cap and scratched his head. "Hello," he said to the woman. "Looks like you found our dog and our pigs."

Scamper and Dash were still joyously climbing all over their mother pig.

The woman was smiling. "Howdy," she said. "I'm hoping you'll be able to explain what just happened, because I'm pretty sure these are the same two little piglets that I

lost more than a week ago. At least, I think they are. And Sadie sure acts like they are."

The big pig had rolled onto her back, and the little pigs were all over her, still squealing and jumping around.

"They are? Well, my wife's rescue got a call that there were two little pigs loose in a truck stop off I-25. When she got there, these little girls were racing around, knocking over clothing racks, and having a grand old time, so she scooped them up and took them back to the animal rescue, and we bottle-fed them until they were old enough to eat on their own. Now we've been out looking for a home for them."

The woman shook her head. "I-25? Truck stop? I wasn't at a truck stop." Suddenly, she gasped. "Wait! I did stop at a rest area. And I think . . . Yes! There was a truck stop across the highway. Somehow these little girls wriggled their way out of the livestock trailer and must've crossed that highway. It's hard to believe, but there can't be any other explanation."

"We've been trying to find a good home for Scamper and Dash," Dad said. "That's what my little girl here named them." Maggie Rose looked up and smiled a little. "We were at your neighbor's place, and they somehow escaped their cage. Her dog, Lily, must have led the pigs straight to your ranch."

"Well, if you're looking for a good home, there isn't a better one than right here with their mommy," the woman said. "I have ducks in my pond, I have that llama, I've got a few cats and an old donkey, and I just love farm animals. I bought Sadie and her two little ones so that they could come here and have a happy life. Scamper and Dash? Those are fine names."

"Scamper is the one with the dark spot on her face," Maggie Rose said.

"I like this ranch," Dad observed. "I especially like the llama."

"Why do you have a llama?" Maggie Rose asked. "Do you ride it?"

"No," the woman replied. "Llamas are pack animals, so I suppose if I did a lot of camping up in the mountains, I'd take him with me and he'd carry my tent and supplies. But no, I just have him for safety."

"Safety?" Maggie Rose asked curiously.

"She's right, Maggie Rose," Dad said. "Llamas are protective. They watch out for their own young, but also for other animals who live with them. Especially a lone male like this one. If a predator showed up, the llama would run to attack it. They don't bite, really, but they can stomp with their legs, and they spit, too. Most predators will back off."

I noticed that my two pig friends had fallen fast asleep on their mother, who was

sprawled on the ground, lying on her side. It looked pretty cozy. I've never napped with a grown pig before, but I was starting to feel tempted.

"So," the woman said, "as you can see, this would be a good home. How much do you want for the pigs?"

"Oh no," Dad said. "I was never going to sell them. We were looking to adopt them out. I'm a game warden, but I spend almost

as much time helping my wife's animal rescue as I do anything else. This is the first
time we've had pigs, though."

"Well," the woman re-
sponded. "You must let me
make a donation to your
wife's rescue operation, at
the very least."

Dad smiled. "That would
be nice," he agreed.

"Could we come visit
Scamper and Dash some-
day?" Maggie Rose asked. "It always makes
me sad when we find a new home for an animal and I never get to see it again."

"Of course!" the woman said, grinning
broadly. "I promise you Scamper and Dash
will never forget you. And they'll definitely
never forget your little dog!"

Maggie Rose walked over to where Sadie
was lying sleepily with her dozing babies.

"Goodbye, Scamper," Maggie Rose said, giving Scamper a big hug. Dash opened her eyes and got to her feet so she wouldn't be left out.

"You, too, Dash," Maggie Rose said, hugging her as well.

We tracked back through the woods, following our scents. As we walked, I could not see or smell Casey anymore, and I wondered if he had flown back to be with Mom and Bryan and Craig.

When we returned to the truck, I saw that the boy and the man who had greeted us were no longer outside. The cage where Scamper and Dash had been wrestling still sat with its door open.

And there was Casey! He was inside the cage, watching us.

"Ree-ree," Casey croaked.

"He must have followed us somehow," Dad marveled. "But he doesn't want to fly all the way back. He wants a ride!" Dad put the cage with Casey in the back of the truck, and we slid in for the long car ride home. As soon as the car started moving, I climbed up and put my feet on the back of the seat so I could look at Casey.

I remembered the pigs. I remembered how happy they had been all the time, how fun it had been to have them with us. I understood now that they had found a new home back with their mother where they belonged. I did not know if I would ever see them again, but it had been wonderful to know them.

Casey was watching me, his head twisting from one side to the other.

I think he agreed.

MORE ABOUT PIGS

Pigs are quite smart. In experiments, they learned to play video games (using special joysticks) and to tell the difference between spearmint, peppermint, and mint. One particular group of pigs even learned to put all their toys away at the end of the day.

Piglets like to play. They chase each other, scamper about, toss their heads, and play-fight with other young pigs.

Pigs are actually quite clean. But they can't sweat to cool down, so they roll in mud to keep themselves from getting too hot. They will also huddle with other pigs to warm up.

Pigs don't lick themselves to keep clean, as dogs and cats do. Instead, they rub against something hard (like a tree, a rock, or a fence post) to scrape dirt off.

Pigs are easier to train than dogs or cats.

There are pigs on every continent of the world except Antarctica.

Pigs are not native to North and South America. Christopher Columbus brought the first pigs to this part of the world in 1493 when his ship landed in Cuba.

A female pig is a sow. A male pig is a boar.

A newborn pig is called a piglet. Mothers nurse their piglets for three to five weeks. Once a young pig is old enough to stop nursing it is known as a shoat.

Wild pigs live in a group called a sounder.

There are usually one to six sows and their children in a sounder.

Wild pigs eat mostly plants, including leaves, roots, berries, grass, seeds, or mushrooms. They will also eat worms, insects, and other small animals if they can get them. On farms, pigs usually eat corn or barley.

Pigs make nests to sleep in. Wild pigs use branches and grass. Farm pigs make piles of hay.

Pigs with curly tails may uncurl them when sleeping.

A pig's sense of smell is as keen as a dog's. Pigs can tell other pigs apart by smell.

Pigs are used to sniff out truffles, a rare and expensive fungus that grows underground.

THE
NOT-SO-STINKY
SKUNK

Dedicated to Georgia Lee Cameron and all the other wonderful people saving lives at Life is Better Rescue in Denver, Colorado. I am very proud of all the work you do!

1

L ily, Lily, Lily!" Mag-
gie Rose said to me.
"We're going camping, Lily!"

Maggie Rose is my girl, and I am her dog.
When she is happy, I am *very* happy. When
she is excited, I am *very* excited. She was obviously excited and happy at this moment, so
I jumped up to put my feet on her knees and
then dropped down to run in circles around
the kitchen. Whatever was going on, it was the
best!

I looked up, wagging, when Mom came in the kitchen carrying a bag. I could smell something delicious in that bag!

"We were out of dog food, so I brought some from the shelter," Mom said. She set the bag down and I padded over to sniff it more carefully. "Would you put it in the pantry, Maggie Rose?"

I was excited when Maggie Rose lifted the bag, grunting a little. "Can you get it?" Mom asked. "It's heavy."

"I got it," my girl replied. I followed her, my nose up, as she put the bag in a closet and shut the door. She skipped back into the kitchen, though I felt that a celebration could include opening the bag at that moment.

"You are such a help with all the animals, Maggie Rose," Mom said, praising her. "I really appreciate everything you do for our rescue operation."

"And Lily!" my girl replied. "Don't forget, she's a rescue, too!"

"And Lily," Mom agreed.

My girl and I ran into the living room, where the floor is softer. We had a very good wrestle with an old towel because we were both so happy.

"Dad's taking us, Lily," Maggie Rose whis-

pered. "We're going up to the mountains. I *never* get to spend time with just Dad!"

I love it when my girl talks to me. I jumped into her lap and licked her ear and under her chin, where she tastes especially delicious.

I didn't know what she was telling me, but I knew it was good.

Maggie Rose flopped down on her back so that I could lie down on top of her and pant in her face.

"Dad says we're going to take care of some prairie dogs first," she told me. I heard the word "dogs" and licked her chin again. Obviously, whatever she was talking about was going to be very good, because she'd said "dogs."

"And then we'll go and camp. You and me and Dad." Maggie Rose hugged me. "Just us!"

"Hey," said a voice that was not as happy as Maggie Rose's. "What do you mean, you're going camping with Dad? Just you?"

Maggie Rose's older brother, Bryan, had come into the room. I ran to sniff Bryan.

"If you're going camping, I want to go, too," Bryan said. "No fair if you get to go and I don't."

"Bryan's right," said another voice. Maggie Rose's oldest brother, Craig, was standing in the doorway, listening to them talk. I went to greet him, and then whipped my head around to stare at my girl.

Something was wrong. Suddenly, just like that, Maggie Rose was not as happy as she'd been a moment ago!

"But Dad said it was just going to be him and me," she said. "You guys are always doing stuff with Dad, and I don't get to go."

"Stuff like what?" Bryan demanded.

I pounced on the old towel and shook it. *This* would make Maggie Rose happy again!

"He goes to your games all the time," she

said, "and takes you to the park to practice soccer and baseball."

"Well, if you did a sport, he'd do that for you, too," Craig pointed out. "You could join the soccer team at school. Or T-ball."

Bryan snorted. "She's too much of a runt to be any good at soccer."

Maggie Rose's back stiffened. I could tell this was some kind of wrestling match going on between her and her brothers. I used to live with my three brothers, before I came to live at Home with my girl, and I remembered wrestling with them.

People sometimes wrestle with words instead of jumping on each other and rolling around in the dirt. I don't really understand how it works, but I can tell when they are wrestling. I can also tell when somebody wins.

Right now, Maggie Rose was wrestling back. But she hadn't won.

"Don't call me a runt," she said. "You're supposed to stop that."

"Yeah, Bryan, knock it off," Craig agreed.

Bryan flopped down on the couch and snorted again.

"And I don't want to play soccer or T-ball. I'm busy most days after school helping Mom at the animal rescue," Maggie Rose went on. "Anyway, I don't see why I should have to play soccer just to spend time with Dad. That's not fair."

"And I don't see why you get some sort of special girl camping trip just for you," Bryan said. "That's not fair, either."

When a dog doesn't understand what people are doing, sometimes the best thing to do is to hunt for treats. I jumped up on the couch to sniff at Bryan's jeans. I could tell that he'd recently had a peanut butter sandwich in one of his pockets.

I pushed my nose as deep into the pocket as

it would go. There was no sandwich in there now, but if I kept sniffing, maybe one would appear.

"Dad!" Bryan called. "Maggie Rose says she's going camping with you."

I pulled my head out of Bryan's pocket to see Dad join us in the living room. I wagged. Mom followed as well, standing just behind Craig in the doorway. She didn't say anything, probably because she was holding a towel. When *I* have a towel, it pretty much takes all my concentration.

"Yes, that's right," Dad agreed.

I could tell that Dad didn't have any peanut butter sandwiches, so I stuck my nose back into Bryan's pocket.

"We want to go, too," Bryan said.

"Yeah, come on, Dad," Craig said. "We haven't been camping since last spring, when it rained the whole time. We should get to go, too. It's not fair if Maggie Rose is the only one."

"But Dad, you said it would just be you and me," Maggie Rose protested.

Her voice sounded so worried that I pulled my head out of Bryan's pocket. I realized I had let her down. To be a good dog, I needed to comfort her, especially since no sandwich had shown up in Bryan's jeans. Something was really bothering her. I jumped to the floor, the peanut butter scent forgotten. Maggie Rose was sitting with her legs crossed. I leaped into her lap and gazed up into her face. What was happening?

"Well," Dad said thoughtfully. "I can see what you boys mean."

"No," my girl moaned. I could see Maggie Rose slump in on herself.

She had lost the wrestling match.

2

Do you mind if your brothers come too, Maggie Rose?" Dad asked.

"But Dad," Maggie Rose said in a sad, soft voice. "I was hoping it would be a father-daughter camping trip."

Dad frowned. Now something was bothering *him*. "Oh," he said.

Maggie Rose turned her face away. A good dog right there in the room, and everyone was unhappy. No one said anything;

they were probably waiting for me to come up with something cheerful. I should have brought in a stick from the yard!

"I'm sorry, Maggie Rose," Dad said.

My girl sighed. "It's okay," she muttered.

Inspired, I flopped on my back and exposed my tummy. A belly rub makes everyone happy!

Craig stirred. I glanced at him. He was watching Maggie Rose carefully. "You know what?" he said suddenly. "Maybe Maggie Rose is right. She can do a father-daughter trip, and then next time, we can do a father-sons camping trip."

"What?" Bryan demanded.

"Sure. We can go to a movie with Mom or something," Craig continued.

"That could work," Mom agreed. "I have a stray cat coming into the rescue with an eye infection I need to treat, but the rest of my day is free. A movie sounds fun."

Maggie Rose brightened, a small grin on her face. I had done it—I had cheered her up!

"I want to go camping," Bryan insisted stubbornly.

"Come on, Bryan," Craig urged.

"No," Bryan said.

"Let's vote," Maggie Rose suggested.

Dad smiled. "Good idea, Maggie Rose."

I had even made Dad happy!

"Who says this time it's father-daughter?" Craig asked.

Everyone held their hand up in the air, except Bryan. He was the only person I hadn't yet managed to make happy. I went to him and put my nose right in his peanut butter pants.

"And who says it's all of us?" Craig asked.

Bryan lifted his hand in the air, and I gazed up at it curiously. If he thought he was going to throw a ball or something, he was going to be disappointed; his hand was empty.

"All right then, Maggie Rose," Dad said. "Just you and me."

"Yay!" Maggie Rose cheered.

I wagged. What a fun day!

"Let's go do something outside, Bryan," Craig suggested. The two of them left the room. Dad leaned down to pet my head, because I was such a good dog who made everyone happy except Bryan, who maybe just needed a sandwich that I would be willing to help him eat.

"I liked how they handled that themselves," Mom observed.

"Me, too," Dad replied. Mom turned and went back toward the kitchen, where all the food is, which I thought was a promising development.

"We have a stop to make along the way," Dad told Maggie Rose. "There's a colony of prairie dogs up near the campground that needs relocating. Someone's putting in a housing development, and the prairie dogs are too close to the new construction. They could get hurt."

My ears perked up and I wagged. There was that word "dogs" again.

"Then we'll head up and pitch a tent, just you and me," Dad concluded.

"And Lily!" Maggie Rose said.

We rolled on the floor and wrestled with the towel some more, and I let her pull it right out of my mouth a few times, so that she'd keep on being that happy.

A few days later, Maggie Rose was very busy putting things into a box made of cloth. She stuffed clothes in there, and her pajamas, and a pair of shoes.

She picked up one of my favorite toys—two old socks that used to belong to Craig before they were mine. They were knotted together to make a long rope.

I lunged. Hooray! We were going to play Pull-on-the-Socks!

I got my teeth into one end of the socks and tugged. Maggie Rose tugged back.

"No, Lily, no!" she kept saying, but she was giggling, so I knew she was as happy to be playing with me as I was to be playing with her. Finally, she whisked the toy out of my mouth.

"No, Lily—I'm trying to pack it in the suitcase, so we'll have something for you to play with!" she told me, and she stuffed the socks into the cloth box along with all the other things.

I sat and stared in confusion. How could we tug on a sock if she was going to put it in that box?

But I soon forgot about it, because Maggie Rose called me out for a car ride in the truck. Rides with my girl are one of my favorite things. Dad sat in the front of the truck. In the back, Maggie Rose rolled the window down a little, so that I could put my nose to the crack and sniff and sniff and sniff.

At first I smelled the city—cars and trucks, with their sour odors of smoke and metal and hot oil; pavement; and all sorts of people living close together, lots with food smells on them. There were dogs, too, and many other animals. The city packed all of these scents into one thick, dense smell.

We drove for a while, and the houses started to be spaced farther and

farther apart. There were more trees and wider stretches of grass. There were more animals out here, too, not just dogs. Sometimes we passed horses or cows in fields, who just stared in jealousy that there was a dog in a car staring back; and sometimes there were other animals that I could not see but only smell, faint on the air.

"I can't wait to see the prairie dogs. They're so cute!" Maggie Rose said eagerly.

Dad nodded. "I think so, too. But they can be a problem."

"What kind of problem?" Maggie Rose asked. "They're so little. It's not like they can hurt somebody."

"Actually, they can," Dad said. "They carry fleas, and fleas can carry diseases. So you and Lily should both stay in the truck."

I put my head in Maggie Rose's lap with a long sigh of contentment.

I love my girl.

"Prairie dogs live in family groups—coteries—so there can be a lot of them. And they're rodents.

They eat seeds and grasses, mostly. They dig tunnels underground. Most people don't want a prairie dog tunnel under their lawn. Or under a field. Sometimes a horse will slip into a prairie dog hole and break a leg."

"Well, maybe people shouldn't build houses where prairie dogs live, then!" Maggie Rose declared, a little fiercely.

Dad shook his head. "Well, people want houses, Maggie. We live in a house, don't we? And horses and cows need fields. What we've got to do—what it's my job to do—is balance out the needs. Try and find a safe place for animals, where they're not going to create a problem for people."

"So we're going to catch them and set them free somewhere else?" Maggie Rose asked.

Dad nodded. "That's the idea. The problem, though, is that prairie dogs are really hard to round up. Today we're going to try something new. If it works, we'll have a safe way to catch them."

"What if it doesn't work?" Maggie Rose asked anxiously. I wagged, thinking that if she was worried about something, we should get Craig's socks out of the cloth box.

Dad didn't answer right away. Then he gave Maggie Rose a serious look. "If this doesn't work, I am not sure we can save the prairie dogs."

3

Maggie Rose's body tightened in a way I knew was a mixture of angry and afraid. I nosed her hand. Dad glanced at her again. "Oh, sorry, honey. I didn't mean to upset you. I think we're going to be fine. Basically, we're going to catch the prairie dogs by vacuum suction."

"What?" Maggie Rose spluttered. She sounded so surprised that I cocked my head at her, staring into her face. "You're going to vacuum up the prairie dogs?" she asked. "Like with a vacuum cleaner?"

I could tell from Dad's voice that he was amused. "Sort of. It's a new technology. It used to be there was no safe way to get rid of a prairie dog coterie. People would have to shoot them or poison them—"

"No!" Maggie Rose cried out.

"Right. No good," Dad agreed. "So someone came up with this idea. It really is a lot like a giant vacuum cleaner. There's a hose that goes into the tunnel and just sucks the prairie dogs right out and into a padded cage."

"Doesn't it hurt them?" Maggie Rose asked. She sounded a little anxious, and I licked her hands to reassure her. "I wouldn't like it if someone pulled the roof off my house and sucked me up!"

"Well, I'm sure it's scary for them," Dad said. "That's partly why I'm going, to make sure no animals get hurt. If it seems too rough, I'll put a stop to it. But if it works, it's really the best thing. Getting the prairie dogs away from humans means everybody can live in peace. So let's cross our fingers."

Maggie Rose still seemed worried. I could not understand it at all. Both of them kept saying "dog," so we must have been going somewhere fun. Probably a dog park! What was there to be worried about in a dog park?

But when the truck came to a stop and Dad climbed out, Maggie Rose and I stayed in the back seat. So clearly, we were not at a dog park at all. I never have to stay in the car at a dog park.

At least Maggie Rose opened the windows so I could see and smell. She clicked my leash on my collar, though, and held it so that I could not jump out.

There were several people walking around outside, and I wanted to sniff them all and

make new friends. Also, there was a fascinating smell drifting toward me on the
breeze. Somewhere close by was a completely
new animal I had never met before.

I wanted to meet that animal very much.
I am very good at meeting animals! I have
met a crow named Casey and two pigs and a
squirrel, plus so many dogs and cats I have
lost count. And a ferret named Freddie, of
course. They are all my friends.

When was I going to get a chance to make
friends with this new animal?

The people gathered together in groups
and talked, and then they walked around and
talked some more. I looked up at Maggie Rose
and whined so that she'd know to let me out.

Maggie Rose stroked my back. "No, Lily,"
she said. "We have to stay here."

I do not like that word, "no."

I perked up; the field was littered with
mounds of dirt with holes in them, and for

just a moment a small head poked
up and then vanished back down.
This was the new animal I could
smell so strongly!

Two of the men outside stuck
a long hose into a hole in the
ground. The other end of the hose
went into a truck that was parked
right next to ours. The back of the
truck had a big window set into
one side so that I could see right
into it. I yawned, not understanding anything.

"Ready!" someone shouted.
Then there was a very loud, rum-
bling *whoosh*. I jumped, startled,
and tried to shake the sound out
of my ears. I wished it would stop,
but it just went on and on!

Dad turned and looked back at

VRRRR

VRRRR

us, probably wondering why we didn't jump
out and run around. He shook his head and
raised his hands.

"Oh no—he says it isn't working, Lily!"
Maggie Rose moaned.

I looked at my girl. Whatever we were doing was not making her happy. I tried to
think of what I could do, but all I could think
of was chicken treats.

"Got one!" shouted a voice. "There it goes!"

Maggie Rose squirmed nearer to the window. "Lily, look!"

I had no idea what she was talking about, though I wagged a little to hear my name. Suddenly, to my surprise, I caught a glimpse of something moving inside the truck near ours. Through the big window, I could see a small furry body drop through the air and plop onto the floor. It immediately jumped up and glanced around. It looked like a big squirrel! As far as I could tell without smelling it, it seemed very surprised.

"They vacuumed one up!" Maggie Rose told me excitedly.

The squirrel in the back of the truck was sniffing at the floor, maybe looking for peanuts. This was a new type of squirrel to me, and I wagged, thinking how much fun we were going to have when Maggie Rose let me join it in the big truck with the window! A moment later it was joined by another, and then another. They all touched noses, like dogs in a dog park, but they did not sniff each other's butts.

"It's like a bounce house!" Maggie Rose told me. She clapped her hands together. She was grinning. "A prairie dog bounce house. Do you think they like bounce houses as much as I do, Lily?"

Yes, I thought to myself. If we weren't going to have chicken treats, I was ready to play with the new squirrels.

Pretty soon, the loud noise stopped. I was relieved. Dad returned to the truck, smiling.

"Got them all, I think," he told Maggie Rose. "No injuries. Looks like this is really going to work!"

Now everyone was happy! This is one of the main jobs of being a dog, and I was glad I had managed to cheer everyone up. I thought it would be an excellent time to break out Craig's socks. A man and a woman, both wearing thick gloves, climbed into the truck where the small plump squirrels had landed. I wished I could go in there, too. I would love to play Chase-Me in a truck full of squirrels!

But it seemed that no one was thinking about how much a good dog would like to play Chase-Me, because in a little while our truck was moving again, and so was the truck with the big windows. They were taking the new squirrels for a car ride!

I squirmed around in Maggie Rose's arms to watch out the back window. She unsnapped my leash so I could move more easily.

I was not sure what we were doing. If these squirrels were going for a car ride, why couldn't they be here in the back seat with my girl and me? We could all sniff out the windows.

"Next stop: a new home for prairie dogs!" Dad said to Maggie Rose.

I wagged. Dad sounded so happy that a dog park seemed like a real possibility!

Finally, the truck came to a stop. We were in

a grassy field. A couple of other cars bumped down the road after us and stopped nearby.

I looked eagerly at Maggie Rose, wagging as hard as I could. We were going to get out now, right? And run with the squirrels?

"Is this where the prairie dogs are going to live, Dad?" Maggie Rose asked.

Dad nodded. "I came out here with some other wardens a couple of days ago, and we dug a new burrow for them," he said. "They need someplace to hide, or hawks or ferrets could get them."

"Ferrets like Freddie? At the shelter?" Maggie Rose asked. "I've never seen Freddie try to hunt any of the other animals. He's friends with Lily!"

Dad put his hand on my head, smoothing my fur, and I wagged. "Sure, but a tame ferret in a cage isn't the same as a wild one, honey," Dad said. "Freddie gets fed every day, so he doesn't have to hunt. There are wild ones out here, though, and prairie dog is on their menu. But with a tunnel to dive into, these little guys should be safe. Let's see how they like their new home!"

Then Dad climbed out, but to my surprise, Maggie Rose didn't. She didn't let me out, either. I barked at the windows to remind her that I had been a good dog in the car for a very long time, and I needed to run around. Peeing would be nice, too. But she didn't open the door. She did, however, lower my window all the way, so I could drink in all the wonderful odors.

Dad walked around to the back of the squirrel truck. He and a woman held sticks with big nets on the end. When he opened the back of the truck, the new squirrels scampered and squeaked inside their room. They seemed unhappy.

Clearly, they needed a good dog to cheer them up. I looked impatiently at Maggie Rose.

When was she going to let me out of the car?

I didn't understand what was going on! Dad and the woman began gently thrusting their sticks into the back of the truck, pulling out netfuls of squirrels. The two humans set all the squirrels on the ground and the little creatures immediately took off running, as if playing Chase-Me. They ran a very short distance to some mounds of dirt. They sniffed the dirt, but mostly they sniffed each other. They seemed confused, which I understood—how do you play Chase-Me without a dog?

Dad came back to us. "They've found the prairie dog town, but they don't want to go in the tunnels for some reason. We're going to have to chase them into the holes, get them used to the idea!"

I wagged.

Dad stood and watched as the rest of the people moved slowly, walking around the confused pack of new squirrels. He groaned when a good number of the little animals started doing the game correctly, dashing a short distance out into the open fields. "Stop!" he called. "This is just making this worse!"

I simply couldn't understand it. The squirrels had bunched up, sniffing each other, trying to figure out when I would come out and play. The people had stopped moving and were standing around with their hands on their hips.

"Laurie," Dad called, "go way around, out

into the field, cut off their escape that way. This is a disaster—we need to get them into the holes! But they have never seen people, and don't understand what we are."

I saw a woman run away and then, after a few moments, curve around until she wound up standing far out in the grass, between us and the squirrels. They saw her, too: they stood up on their rear legs, trying to see what she was up to.

I couldn't wait any longer. I squirmed and twisted and slipped out of Maggie Rose's hands. Then I leaped for the open window.

Time to play!

"Lily, come back!" Maggie Rose shrieked.

5

As soon as I hit the ground, I started running straight toward the cluster of squirrels, so happy to finally be playing! They reacted by milling around for a moment and then dashing in all directions.

"No, Lily!" Maggie Rose wailed.

I was almost on top of a squirrel, and then it vanished! It had darted down into a hole. I turned to pursue another, and it dove into the ground as well. What? These squirrels

weren't climbing trees, but they were playing unfairly anyway. Within moments, they
were all gone!

I always think squirrels are going to do
Chase-Me correctly, but I get fooled every
time.

Dad came over and reached down and I
wagged. He picked me up in his big, thick
gloves and carried me over to the truck.
"Well, I should be angry with you that you

let Lily escape," he told Maggie Rose as she opened the door, "but it turns out she was just what we needed. The prairie dogs didn't understand when they saw people coming to try to herd them, but they recognized a predator when they saw one, and followed their instincts right into their new homes!"

"Oh, Lily would never hurt any of them."

"Right," Dad agreed. "But they don't know that."

Dad took me to the back of the truck, raised the door, and pulled out a hose.

"What are you doing?" my girl asked him.

"I don't think Lily has any fleas on her, but we can't take that chance. I have flea shampoo, and I am going to bathe her right now with this water tank I always carry."

I was wagging until Dad started giving me a bath, and then I was not wagging. A bath? After I had been such a good dog?

Sometimes I just do not understand people.

Dad used miserably stinky liquid on me, and I sneezed, and then he poured water on me and toweled me down. I liked the towel but nothing else. Finally, he took me to Maggie Rose and laid me in her lap.

"I'm watching the prairie dogs, Dad! They keep coming up to look around, and a couple are digging in the grass," Maggie Rose said as Dad started the truck.

"It worked like a charm. Great to have a new way of moving those little guys without hurting them!" Dad said happily.

I settled onto Maggie Rose's lap for a nap, but I woke up when the truck stopped. I figured we were Home again, or maybe at Work, where I have so many friends—Brewster the dog, Freddie the ferret, and all the other cats and dogs who visit for a while and then leave with their new people.

But where we were—it did not smell like Home or Work. The scent of this place wafted in through the open windows, and it smelled full of plants and living things. It smelled *wild*.

"Come and see the campsite, Lily!" Maggie Rose said, and she held the door open for me.

We were on a small, flat patch of ground surrounded by trees—towering trees, more and bigger than I had ever seen in one place before. Through a couple of the trees I could see and smell a big patch of water. Next to us was the truck, and a sooty circle surrounded by rocks, and a flat table with benches alongside it, and a strange sort of house made of cloth that Dad was tugging on.

What *was* this place?

Nose to the dirt, I dashed around eagerly, pulling Maggie Rose behind me on my leash. Other people had walked over this area, but not very many. More animals than people had been here. Some of the scents I recognized, like squirrels (tree squirrels, not hole-in-the-ground squirrels) and deer.

Were we going to stay here? Was this our new Home? What about Mom and Bryan and Craig? What about Work, with all my animal friends? Wouldn't they miss me? I would certainly miss them!

"Oh, Lily, you look worried," Maggie Rose said. She got down on her knees to scratch my back and rub my ears. "Don't worry, you'll like camping. It's going to be fun. Fun, Lily!"

So then I knew that, whatever was happening, it was going to be good. Maggie Rose was happy. That proved it.

"I feel kind of bad that the boys don't get to see this," Maggie Rose said, looking up at Dad. "They would really love this place."

Dad had some big pieces of wood in his arms. He dropped them next to the sooty circle on the ground.

"You've got a big heart, Maggie Rose," he said. "And we'll come back with the boys another day. But this time is for you and me."

I gnawed on a stick while Maggie Rose and Dad pulled things from the car and put them inside the cloth house. Then Dad played with his wood that he had put in the sooty circle on the ground. Before too long, the sharp smell of smoke pushed up into the air, with bright flames licking out from the sticks.

Sometimes at Home I had seen a fire in the fireplace, but this was new! It seemed more exciting to have a fire out in the open, not stuck behind a screen in the wall. We were having a wonderful time, even if I wasn't sure what we were doing. I sat and scratched behind my ear with a rear paw.

I *really* liked the open fire when Maggie Rose and Dad put hot dogs on sticks and stuck them into the flames. That smelled so marvelous that I drooled in the dirt! I sat

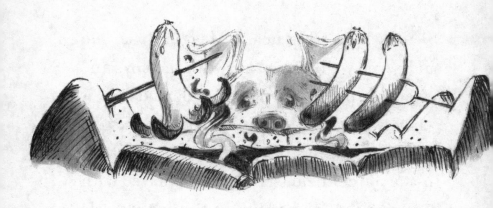

and watched intently as Maggie Rose put her hot dog in bread, sprayed it with something that had a sweet odor, and began eating.

I concentrated on staring at Maggie Rose, letting her know with my gaze that I would very much appreciate a piece of hot dog. I was being a good dog. Would she give me one?

6

"Here, Lily," Maggie Rose said to me. She extended a big chunk of hot dog toward me, and I delicately lifted it from her fingers. This was how I knew my girl loved me, and that I was indeed a good dog who deserved a piece of hot dog, and hopefully another one.

After the sky turned dark, Dad and Maggie Rose and I climbed inside the cloth house.

It was a strange place! There were no beds. Maggie Rose lay down on the floor and snuggled into a silky kind of blanket that was a little like the bags Mom and Dad carried food in. Dad lay down beside her in his own bag. There was no bag for a dog.

I was so puzzled I flung myself on my girl, panting into her face.

"Ugh, Lily, calm down!" Maggie Rose said. She put an arm around me and tugged me down between her and Dad. "You sleep here, okay, Lily? Sleep right here."

Maggie Rose lay still, and after a while I could tell from her breathing that she was sleeping. Dad, too.

But I was wide awake. All the smells of the outdoors came drifting into the cloth house, and I could hear birds calling, small animals scurrying, and something bigger clomping through the bushes.

I squirmed up to lick Maggie Rose's face, wanting her awake so that she could experience all this with me.

"Mmmmmph. Lily. No," Maggie Rose said sleepily.

That word again. "No." I licked Maggie Rose's ear. Why wouldn't she wake up? Surely we weren't going to just lie here, with all the animal scents and sounds on the other side of the cloth walls.

"Lily. Sleep. Now," Maggie Rose mumbled.

So I had to lie there, the only one awake.

What was going on?

In the morning I decided my confusion didn't matter, because everything was so much fun!

First, Dad cooked breakfast over the fire. Maggie Rose put my regular food in my bowl for me, but she also let me have some of her scrambled eggs with bacon. The bacon was a little burned, but I did not care at all. I will eat bacon under all circumstances.

Then she took me for a walk in the woods,

but she did not put on my leash. And I had never smelled so many interesting smells in one place. Rocks! Moss! Leaves! Sticks! Animal poop!

And even more exciting were the animals who had left the poop. Animal scents were everywhere! They had walked over the ground, and they had left scratches in the dirt and pee under the bushes.

I could hardly believe how marvelous it was! Yes, I missed Mom and Casey and Brewster and Craig and Bryan with his peanut butter pockets, but this place was the best, and as far as I was concerned they should all come to live with us here and sleep in the cloth room.

The only thing that could have made it better was if some of these animals had come out to play. But they seemed to be shy. Some animals are shy at first, but I've made friends with nearly all of them in the end. If they became really good friends, I thought, they could sleep in the cloth room with the rest of us.

Maggie Rose led me down a path toward the glimmering water I had glimpsed yesterday.

I was surprised when we arrived there. I was used to seeing the water in my bowl, and I'd watched Maggie Rose fill up the tub at Home with water and get in it. That was called a "bath," and I usually left the room as soon as I heard the word, because I did not want to get involved in such matters. My girl's bath-water had bubbles in it that smelled strange and tasted worse. My baths, like the one I'd just had, had fewer bubbles and smelled absolutely awful.

There is no reason for anyone to ever take a bath that a dog can understand.

This water, though, was different. For one thing, it was huge! There was much more water than would ever fit into my bowl, or even into Maggie Rose's tub.

It did not have bubbles in it, either. Instead, there were plants growing in it. I took a tentative drink, then returned to my girl's side. Then, in the bushes behind her,

I caught a new scent. I stopped and sniffed hard.

An animal! A new friend! I could hear it now. It made a rustling sound. It was coming closer! It had stopped being shy and was ready to play!

A slender, dark head with two glistening eyes poked out of the bush behind Maggie Rose. My new friend was small, about the same size as Freddie, my friend the ferret, and I could smell that she was female. I could also smell that she was not a dog. As she emerged from the shrubs, I saw that she was all black, except for two long white stripes down her back.

Another new type of squirrel? I already knew that dogs came in all sizes and shapes, but I'd never before considered that squirrels might try to be like dogs, and be different from each other as well.

A striped squirrel! How exciting! Maybe

this one would play Chase-Me fairly. I bowed
down with my front legs low, my rump high,
and my tail waving, to let my new squirrel
friend know I was ready.

The squirrel made a funny kind of grunting sound, turned, and waddled back into
the bush.

Time to chase!

"Lily! Where are you going?" Maggie Rose shouted as I plowed through the bush. "Come back! That's a skunk!"

7

Twigs and leaves slapped me, but I struggled through. On the other side, right by a mossy log, was my new friend. She peered at me and then turned so her butt was facing me.

Obviously, this was a squirrel who understood the polite way to introduce herself to a dog. I wanted to be polite as well, so I trotted up to give her butt a good sniff. My new friend lifted up her tail so I could smell better. This

was also new information, that some squirrels wanted so much to be like dogs that they
had learned how to act like us.

I could hear Maggie Rose trying to come
through the bush after us. "Dad! Lily ran
after a skunk!" she called.

"No, Lily!" Dad shouted.

Why would anyone say "No!" about meeting a new friend? People should really think

harder about how they use that word. Other than "bath," it was the worst thing humans could ever say. I sniffed my new friend's butt more deeply.

"Call her! We can't let her get sprayed by that skunk, Maggie Rose!" Dad yelled.

"Lily, come here! Get away from the skunk!" my girl called out.

There were two words in that sentence that I knew—"Lily" and "come." And Maggie Rose was saying a new word I had never heard before. Dad had said that word, too.

"Skunk." They were saying "skunk."

Perhaps they meant that my new friend was called skunk, not squirrel. Maybe that's why it didn't run up a tree or down a hole or into a giant hose.

I left the skunk and ran toward my girl, because she'd said "come." I always go to her when she says that.

Well, most of the time.

Some of the time, anyway.

Oddly, as I approached, wagging happily, Maggie Rose did not seem glad to see me. She backed away as I came closer. What was wrong?

"Great," Dad groaned. "Lily got sprayed by that skunk. Take her down to the pond, Maggie Rose. I've still got some shampoo in the truck. I'll go fetch it. You get her fur wet. But try not to let her rub against you, or we'll have to clean you, too."

"Come on, Lily," Maggie Rose urged, moving backward toward the big water. "Lily, follow me—no, don't touch me!" She skipped out of my way. "Come, Lily!"

This was an extremely confusing game. She was calling me, but then when I obeyed, she said "no." Did she want me close to her or not? But I followed her, because she's my girl.

Maggie Rose kicked off her shoes and

waded right into the water. I sat on the shore and watched curiously. She waded up to her knees and then called to me. "Lily, come!"

So now she wanted me near her again. I splashed happily into the water.

Maggie Rose backed away from me. "It's so cold!" she exclaimed. She scooped up a handful of water and tossed it at me. "Better get you wet. Here, Lily! We need to give you a bath!"

I froze. A bath? Another *bath*? Was that why we were here? That couldn't be true, could it?

I shook my head to get rid of the water and spotted something floating right behind my girl. A stick! A stick would take her mind off the whole bath subject. I lunged at it. It felt funny, trying to run in the heavy water. I pushed through it and heaved myself forward.

Suddenly there was no more sand under

my paws. It had dropped away, and all I could touch was water. It was like jumping into one of the holes Craig and Bryan sometimes dug in the field.

I was sinking.

This was very interesting. I had never been underneath water before. I kept trying to run, but my running was not taking me anywhere. My paws brushed pebbles and then I was standing, looking up, where the sun was acting very crazy, dancing and bobbing at the surface of the water.

I could faintly hear Maggie Rose calling, "Lily! Lily!" I hoped she would soon realize that I couldn't run to her. I was a good dog who always came when I was called, but not now!

I couldn't even really see my girl.

I couldn't smell her.

I could hardly hear her.

I saw her wobble and jump as she waded toward me. My girl's hands plunged through the clear water to grab me and pull me up to the surface. "Lily! I've got you!" she gasped.

She held me tight to her chest. She was struggling, as if she were trying to run just as I had been. But she wasn't getting anywhere.

The water was nearly over my head. Only my nose and eyes were out. I was glad about my nose, because I realized now that I had not been able to breathe during that underwater time.

Maggie Rose was up to her neck, too. Her head was tipped back in the water so that just her face was out. "Dad!" she shouted.

Dad came running down the path and leaped into the water with us. Now we were all playing this strange water game.

People usually decide what dogs are going to do, but in my opinion, there are other games that are more fun. Like Chase-Me. Or Pull-on-Craig's-Socks.

Dad grabbed Maggie Rose and me together. "I've got you both." He picked us up and carried us to the shore. Then he sat down on a big log with my girl on his lap, hugging her.

I squirmed away and ran in a few circles and tried to shake the water out of my fur. What were we going to do next? Maybe it would involve bacon.

My girl was shivering. "You're okay. You're okay," Dad told her. "Lily's okay, too."

"I was scared," Maggie Rose replied weakly. "Lily just sank. I thought she'd dog paddle."

"Not all dogs can swim," Dad told her. "Lily's a pit bull mix, and pits are pretty heavy. All that muscle. They can't float, so some of them can't doggy paddle. Don't go in after her again, Maggie Rose, hear me? Call for me. Got it?"

Maggie Rose nodded.

Dad hugged her tightly. Then he laughed just a little bit. "Great. We're all going to smell like skunk now."

Maggie Rose laughed a little, too.

I wagged.

Dad lifted his hands to his face and smelled them.

He frowned.

8

ad put his face in
Maggie Rose's hair
and inhaled deeply through his nose.

This was interesting! I watched closely.
I have never understood why people do not
sniff things more. They miss so many wonderful scents.

"You don't smell like skunk, either," he
said. "Lily! Lily, come!"

Maggie Rose wiggled off of Dad's lap, and

I trotted over to him. Maybe it would be my turn on Dad's lap now.

But Dad put out a hand to stop me before I could snuggle. He put his nose in my fur. He sniffed. I wagged and sniffed him back. I wondered if I should turn around so he could sniff under my tail.

"No skunk smell at all!" Dad declared.

"Maybe the skunk missed Lily?" Maggie Rose suggested.

"Couldn't have. She had her nose right in the skunk's butt, and I saw it lift up its tail and aim right at her. Your dog should have gotten a full blast of skunk right in her face. A skunk's spray is the only way it can protect itself. They're not fast, they don't have big teeth, and they can't climb trees. All they can do is squirt that awful smell. And it works! Even bigger animals will back right off if a skunk lifts up its tail. So how come Lily doesn't stink?"

My girl was shivering. "I don't know."

"You're both way too cold to sit around talking about skunks!" Dad decided. "Come on. We've got to get you dry."

We went back to the place where we'd spent the night, and Dad put more wood on the fire. I wagged, remembering the bacon from breakfast. Maggie Rose crawled into the cloth house and came out again with dry clothes on. She carried a towel that she used to rub me all over.

It felt good! I wiggled and jumped. But I was still trembling, and Maggie Rose was, too.

"Sit right by the fire," Dad said. "Here." He went into the cloth house, too, and came out with a blanket that he wrapped around my girl.

"But what about Lily?" Maggie Rose asked. "She's cold, too."

"She's got fur. She'll be okay."

Maggie Rose thought for a moment. "I know!" She shook off the blanket and climbed into the cloth house. Was this a new people game, crawling in and out of the cloth house? She came back out with a puffy coat in her hand. She draped the coat over my back. Then she picked up my front legs, one at a time, and stuffed them into the arms of the coat.

I let her do this, because I love her. Then I stood up and shook as hard as I could.

The coat did not fall off. But the hood flopped forward over my eyes. I shook my head hard to make it go away. It only flopped down farther until it hung over my nose.

My girl was giggling. Dad was laughing, too.

None of this could possibly make sense to a dog.

Dad said, "Once you two are all warmed up, there's something we've got to do."

"What, Dad?" Maggie Rose asked.

"Find that skunk."

In a little while, Maggie Rose figured out that I did not want to be in her coat and took it off me. She rubbed her hair hard with the towel and hung it up on a rope stretched between two trees. "Ready!" she told Dad.

"Great," Dad said. "If that skunk actually

can't spray, it can't defend itself. And we can't leave it out here like that. So let's see if Lily can track it down."

"Find the skunk, Lily!" Maggie Rose said to me.

I sat down on the ground and looked up at her. What game were we playing now?

Maggie Rose hurried off down the path toward the water. I followed, of course. When she reached the bush where I had met my black-and-white friend, she stopped. She pointed at the thick shrubs.

"Skunk, Lily!" she said. "Find the skunk!"

Clearly, Maggie Rose wanted me to do something. I tried to think what that might be. Some sort of treat would probably help me figure it out. That bacon would be best.

"Find the skunk!"

Skunk. She and Dad had said that word earlier, before Maggie Rose and I had played

the strange game in the water. Were we playing another game now?

The way Maggie Rose was saying "find the
skunk!" reminded me of being in the backyard, when she would say, "find the ball!"
When she said that, I would run around until I found a ball and bring it to her.

Maybe I was supposed to find the skunk!

No, that didn't seem right. I gazed at my
girl's face.

"Find the skunk! The skunk!" she urged.

I'd never heard "skunk" before, and now
it seemed like all anyone wanted to say. I
looked around. No skunk. I poked my head
into the bush. I couldn't see any skunk there,
either.

But I could smell it. I put my nose down to
the ground and sniffed. I pushed through the
shrubs and followed the skunk's trail, right
to the mossy log where I had been treated to a

good sniff of her butt. When I had left to play in the water with Maggie Rose, the skunk had climbed over the log and wandered off among the trees.

I clambered right over the log and followed her scent trail.

9

Maggie Rose and Dad followed me as I tracked that skunk across the dirt, around trees, and through patches of dry grass. We were all playing Chase-the-Skunk!

I hoped skunks understood Chase-Me better than squirrels did, and that the skunk would not ruin the game by running up a tree or down a hole or into a loud hose.

There were many interesting animal scents distracting me from that skunk, now that I had my nose to the ground. My girl and Dad were having trouble keeping up, so I felt free to check some of them out. Wait, what was this? A male dog had been here recently. I sniffed carefully.

"Lily! Find the skunk!" Maggie Rose said urgently as she came up behind me.

"Did you lose the trail, Lily?" Dad asked.

I heard my name, and I heard "skunk," which reminded me what we were doing. I plunged off again. I felt a bit like a bad dog for having stopped to sniff the male dog scent, but it was actually his fault, not mine. Male dogs just don't always understand what is important.

I was getting closer, I could tell—the skunk smell was so strong now that I knew Maggie Rose and Dad could probably smell her as well. Should I wait and let them find the skunk, instead?

I was going to do just that when I scrambled over a thick root and plopped down on the other side. There she was! The skunk!

She was clawing at a rotten log on the ground. She stuck her face into the crumbled bit of wood and snapped up something wiggly between her teeth.

Then she saw me. She lifted her tail high, lowered her head, and shifted her weight from foot to foot. She wanted to play! I should have brought Craig's socks.

The skunk backed up and spun around to show me her butt. I'd already sniffed it once, but I didn't want to be rude, so I did it again.

Dad and Maggie Rose were right behind me. I glanced over and saw Dad take something out of Maggie Rose's backpack—a sort of thin cloth net. He threw it forward. It had a weight at each corner, so it flattened out as it sailed through the air.

The net flopped to the ground over the skunk and me, covering us both.

Today I'd had a coat on me, and now I was wearing a net. This was very strange, and not how I usually played.

Enough light was coming through the thin cloth that I could still see the skunk. She did not seem happy. I could tell that she was startled and afraid and she wanted to run, but the net was trapping us both.

I wagged at the skunk, so she'd know we were friends. She backed away from me a little, but she didn't have much space to move.

"Stay there," I heard Dad tell Maggie Rose. Then he came closer. In a moment his big hands pushed through the cloth and scooped that skunk right up—still wrapped tight in the thin net.

I was concerned for my new friend. I wished I knew a way to tell her that, with Dad holding her, she was safe.

The skunk wriggled and bit at the net as Dad carried her to the back of the truck.

I followed, my nose up to smell my new friend. Dad lifted the back of the truck and opened the dog crate there. He plopped the skunk inside, pulled away the thin netting, and shut the door.

"Phew!" Dad said. "That went easier than I expected."

"Can we put Lily in the back, too? She always helps with scared animals," my girl asked. I wagged at my name.

"Well, sure—we can try it, but if it makes

the situation worse, we'll need to pull your dog right back out."

Dad lifted me up and set me next to the dog crate. I peered in through the wire mesh door. The skunk was huddled in a corner. I could tell she was in no mood to play. Sometimes it's like that when I meet new friends.

I flopped down near the crate so that the skunk would see I was no threat. I watched her carefully to see if she understood.

"Look how calm Lily is," Dad said. He sounded a little surprised. "I think she's actually helping the skunk stay calm, too."

"Of course Lily's helping," said Maggie Rose. "She's a rescue dog. It's what she does."

"She's amazing," Dad said. "Maggie Rose, I'm afraid we have to cut our camping trip short. We've got to get this skunk down to your mother. She can tell if the skunk really can't spray scent. If she can't, maybe there's something your mom can do."

"What if Mom can't fix it?" my girl wondered.

Dad was silent for a moment. "Then I don't know if there's anything to help the skunk, honey."

"Mom will fix it," my girl said urgently. "She *has* to!"

Maggie Rose and Dad became very busy, packing things and moving them and putting them in the back of the truck. Dad picked up the box with the bacon in it, and even though we could all smell it in there, he didn't offer me any, which I found baffling.

After it was all over, Maggie Rose reached over and lifted me away from the skunk.

I whined a little. I could tell the skunk was still afraid, and I did not like to leave a new friend who was frightened and alone.

Maggie Rose carried me around to the back seat of the truck and climbed in with me. Another car ride!

I hoped that my new skunk friend liked car rides as much as I did.

10

The skunk did not like the car ride. I could smell her back there in the crate, and she smelled like fear.

We drove all the way to Work. I love Work! On most of the days when Maggie Rose says, "I have to go to school now. Bye, Lily!" I go to Work with Mom.

At Work there are lots of other animals— dogs and cats and kittens and puppies. Once a crow came to stay with us. His name is Casey, and he became one of my best friends.

Another friend is an old dog named Brewster, who is probably the best nap-taker I have ever met.

I wondered what games I would play with my new friend the skunk. So far she had only seemed interested in Sniff-My-Butt.

Dad carried the skunk into Work and put the crate down on the floor. Then he and Mom talked while Maggie Rose and I listened carefully to see if any treats were mentioned. Mom put on a pair of heavy gloves and knelt down to open up the skunk's crate. She reached in and wrapped up the skunk in a piece of thick, tough cloth.

I wondered why both Mom and Dad seemed to think it was a good idea to play a game called Wrap-the-Skunk.

The skunk squirmed and tried to bite. I could smell that she was very frightened. "She's a young one," Mom remarked. Maggie Rose and I waited while Mom looked at the skunk very carefully.

"I think you are exactly right," Mom said to Dad with a sigh. Very gently, she put the skunk back into her crate and pulled away the sheet. "She has no scent glands. As far as I can tell, she was born that way."

"She can't spray?" Dad asked.

Mom shook her head. "She's a stinkless skunk."

Dad's shoulders slumped. "That means she has no defenses at all. There's no way she can survive in the wild."

Maggie Rose took me near the skunk's crate. She set me down. "Go on, Lily," she whispered to me. "Do your job. Make her feel better."

I put my nose to the crate door. I sniffed. The skunk stayed far back in a corner and did not come to touch noses with me.

This was bad. This skunk was very afraid.

Dad started talking to his phone, and Mom went to a desk to look at some papers. Humans like looking at papers. I do not know why. They don't smell or taste interesting at all. Maggie Rose went to the back door and opened it, and wonderful scents drifted in on the warm air. My girl raised her face to the sun and closed her eyes and smiled.

There was a rustle of wings in the air, and something flew in through the open door and landed on top of my head. I felt claws pricking through my fur.

"Ree-ree," a voice croaked. "Ree-ree."

It was my friend Casey! Crows can talk better than dogs, but not as well as people. "Ree-ree" was his way of saying "Lily." Or maybe it was his way of saying "Hello." Or "We should have chicken treats." I am a dog and have too many things going on to try to learn how to understand bird. But I was very happy, and I wagged.

Casey sometimes likes to take rides on my head, so I circled the skunk's crate. Then I went back to the crate door.

The skunk had stirred from her corner. She had come over to the door, and was crouching down low to see what was happening.

Probably she had never seen a crow ride on a dog's head before. A lot of people—and animals, too—are interested when Casey and I do this.

I sat down. Casey stayed on my head. He leaned forward a bit to peer at the skunk. The skunk peered back.

I hoped the skunk was starting to understand that living at Work would be fun. She would get to play with Casey. She would get to play with me. She could nap with Brewster.

"Look, Mom," Maggie Rose said softly. "Lily's doing her job, and Casey's helping!"

"You're right," Mom said, just as softly.

"I've never seen a wild animal calm down so quickly. Sometimes when animals are frightened, seeing something completely unexpected takes their mind off what's scaring them. Like a bird on a dog's head!"

Mom picked up the skunk, and I followed her as she took the little crate inside a kennel. Kennels have a cement floor, a bed to lie on, and dishes full of food.

Mom left me with the skunk crate in the kennel, shutting the gate behind her. What were we doing now?

Casey had flown off my head by then, but he flapped over to the kennel and gripped the wires with both feet so he could gaze down at the skunk. He was as interested as I was.

"Keep an eye on them, Maggie Rose," Mom said. "Don't open the crate, though. Just because that skunk can't spray you doesn't mean she can't bite you."

I sat down beside the crate. Being inside the kennel made me remember my early days, when I had lived in a kennel like this with my mother and my three brothers. That was before I went Home to live with Maggie Rose.

I guessed that the skunk would do the same thing. She would live here in the kennel for a while, and then she'd go Home with us. We'd both eat out of our bowls in the kitchen, and sleep pressed against Maggie Rose's legs in her bed.

"Stinkerbelle," Maggie Rose said to Dad later. "I'm going to name the skunk Stinkerbelle."

"That's a good name," Dad said with a smile.

"If Stinkerbelle can't live in the wild, what are we going to do with her?"

"I don't know, Maggie Rose. I just don't know."

Every day at Work, Maggie Rose would let me into the skunk's kennel. My girl called the skunk Stinkerbelle, so I knew that was the skunk's name. People always know names, even before the animals themselves do. I didn't know I was Lily until Maggie Rose told me.

Inside the kennel was the skunk's crate. The door was open. Stinkerbelle seemed curious about me, but not enough to come out right away. Sometimes she sniffed out the open door, watching me. Casey was often in the kennel, too.

She finally crept out of her small crate one morning. Eyeing me carefully, she waddled over to her bowl and poked her nose into it. There were a lot of different things in that bowl—some soft meat, pieces of broccoli, and chunks of apple. I didn't like the apples or the broccoli, and I didn't see what Stinkerbelle saw in them, but Casey seemed to enjoy them. He would sometimes take one and peck at it until it was gone.

I treated Stinkerbelle as I would a very scared kitten, and just let her become used to me being there. She seemed afraid of me, but was always very interested in Casey. And Casey was always interested in the skunk. Maybe they liked each other because they were each a deep, glossy black, with shiny black eyes.

Friends play with each other a lot, and different friends play different games. With other dogs I might play Get-the-Ball-First or Steal-the-Stick. Cats were pretty good at Chase-Me. Sometimes we played Wrestling.

Casey and I played Sit-on-Lily's-Head a lot.

The skunk, though? I tried bringing a ball into the kennel with me, but she was unimpressed. I shook Craig's old socks, and she just stared at me, amazed. I tried to picture the skunk playing Sit-on-Lily's-Head, but it didn't seem likely.

It did seem that the more time I spent with

Stinkerbelle, the more comfortable she became. Eventually she forgot she was afraid and would sniff me all over, and sniff all over the kennel, and even went up to Casey to sniff.

Casey didn't sniff back. Crows just don't seem to be interested in that sort of thing.

Then Stinkerbelle curled up on her bed, so I curled up with her. I thought Maggie Rose should let Brewster in to sleep with us.

"I have good news," Dad said at breakfast one morning. I was crouched by Bryan's chair, because Bryan is the most likely to drop a piece of food on the floor. I like Bryan very much at mealtimes.

"You're going to let me have that electric skateboard?" Craig guessed.

"Of course not," Dad replied. Craig's legs kicked a little under the table.

"We're going to build a swimming pool?" Bryan suggested.

"A what?" Dad sputtered. Mom started laughing.

"Jason's parents are putting in a pool," Bryan pointed out.

"Everyone, stop talking," Dad said.

"Does it have to do with animals?" Maggie Rose asked. Bryan dropped a piece of toast and I pounced.

"Yes!"

"With the skunk?" my girl guessed.

"Right again, Maggie Rose!" Dad replied.

"We're getting an electric skateboard for the skunk?" Craig asked, sounding surprised.

Dad groaned.

"The skunk's getting a swimming pool?" Bryan demanded.

Now everyone was laughing.

"No. Thanks for the great ideas, but we're taking the skunk to the wildlife sanctuary," Dad went on. "Want to come, Maggie Rose? Lily too, of course. Your mom said Lily and the skunk have really bonded."

"They have," Mom affirmed.

Maggie Rose nodded. Then she looked around the table.

"Can Craig and Bryan come, too?" she asked.

Dad raised his eyebrows.

"Nice of you to think of the boys, Maggie Rose," he said. "Isn't it, you two? Do you guys want to come?"

"Sure," Craig said. "You did good helping to save it, Maggie Rose." Under the table, I saw his toe nudge Bryan's foot. "Hey Bryan, didn't Maggie Rose do a good job with the skunk?"

"Yeah," Bryan muttered.

"It was Lily who found the skunk," Maggie Rose said. "She's really the one who saved it."

A bit of scrambled egg slipped off Bryan's fork and hit the floor. I jumped on it. Mine!

After breakfast was over, we all went for a car ride. All meaning *all* of us! We climbed into the big car that can hold our whole family. Mom and Dad sat in the front. Craig and Bryan had the two middle seats. And Maggie Rose and I had the back seat to ourselves.

The first stop on the car ride was to Work. The whole family didn't often go to Work together. I pranced in with my tail wagging hard, excited to be with my family and my animal friends at the same time. Brewster, who always stays at Work, came stiffly out of his kennel with his tail wagging and sniffed at Craig and Bryan. Maggie Rose dropped down on her knees to give him a hug.

Casey croaked "Ree-ree," from the top of a stack of crates that held a mother cat and her three new kittens. The kittens were too young to come out and play yet, and the

mother hissed at Casey, so Dad shooed him off the crates. Casey flew over Bryan's head (Bryan ducked) and perched on a bookshelf on the other side of the room.

Mom brought Stinker-belle out in the crate. I went up and stuck my nose through the wire.

The skunk was hud-dled in a corner, and she seemed unhappy. But when she saw me, she jumped to her feet and waddled over to touch her nose to mine.

"Lily really is amaz-ing," Mom said. "I'm glad she's here. This will be much less stressful for the skunk with a friend nearby."

I heard wings overhead, and Casey swooped down to perch on the skunk's crate.

"Say goodbye to Stinkerbelle, Casey," Maggie Rose said.

Bryan snorted. "Stinkerbelle? Seriously?"

The skunk lifted her nose toward the roof of her crate. Casey lowered his beak and peered in at her.

"Look, they're really saying goodbye!" Maggie Rose exclaimed. Bryan rolled his eyes.

Dad picked up the skunk's crate and carried it to the car. He put it on the floor of the back seat where Maggie Rose and I were sitting. I could tell that the skunk was scared when the big car started to move, so I hopped down to be close to her.

I sat near the crate and leaned against the wire, so that the skunk could feel my fur. She leaned against me from the other side, and I knew that it made her feel safer.

Another car ride! I wondered where we were going now. Were we going to see more squirrels get sucked into a hose?

I hoped not. I didn't think my skunk friend would enjoy that at all.

12

When the car stopped moving, Maggie Rose put on my leash and took me out. We were in a parking lot with lots of cars and trucks, but the scents filling my nose were not metal and oil and gas. They were animals. Many animals, and they were very near.

Not dogs, though. I was the only dog.

There were squirrels, of course. (There seem to be squirrels everywhere.) And people.

I could definitely smell people. Deer, too—that was a smell I knew.

But the other smells—I couldn't identify them. I'd encountered some of them before, though. When Maggie Rose and Dad and I had been sleeping in the little cloth house, I'd smelled some of these odors in the woods. They'd been rubbed on the trees or were drifting on the air.

Animals. Big ones and little ones.

"Wait until you see this place," Dad said as we walked across the parking lot. "They have thousands of acres, and they have huge enclosures for all the animals they protect. They've got bears, lions, tigers. . . ."

"Tigers!" said Bryan. "I want to see the tigers."

"We will, after we drop off the skunk."

"Why do they have tigers, though?" asked Maggie Rose. "Did they bring them from India or China?"

"No, they're not a zoo. That's why I like this place so much," Dad explained. "They take in animals that can't live in the wild for some reason, or ones that have been kept as pets or in shows."

"Nobody should keep animals like that!" Maggie Rose said angrily.

"You're right," Dad agreed. "Nobody should keep wild animals as pets at all. Those animals can't always be released back into the wild—they never learned to hunt. So they come here."

"That's like Stinkerbelle," Maggie Rose said. "She can't live in the wild. . . ."

"So she can live here," Dad finished. He looked down at my skunk friend in her crate. "Welcome home, Stinkerbelle."

We walked in through a big gate, and Dad shook hands with a man who had hair underneath his nose and who smelled like coffee and ham and mustard. He lived with two different dogs. I could tell when I sniffed his shoes.

"Oh," said the man, looking down at me. "We don't usually allow dogs."

"Lily has a job to do," Maggie Rose said firmly. I wagged to hear my name, and wondered if we were going to play soon. "She helps Stinkerbelle stay calm."

The man looked surprised. Mom nodded. "My daughter's right."

"Fair enough." Nose-Hair Man led us along hard paths set into the dirt. There were fences on either side, and on either side of the wire were big stretches of grass.

Something was sleeping behind and alongside one of the fences, in a sunny spot. It looked like a huge pile of brown fur. Was it a dog? It was bigger than any dog I'd ever seen. And it didn't smell doglike.

It smelled . . . big. And male. And inter-esting! I pulled on the leash, trying to tug Maggie Rose toward the heap of fur.

"No, Lily—you can't sniff a bear!" she said, pulling me back.

I whined with frustration. The heap of fur made a snorting sound and rolled over, stretched four paws, and collapsed back into sleep again.

"That's Winston," said Nose-Hair Man. "He likes nothing better than a nap in a sunny spot. And here's the home we've made for your skunk!"

He stopped by a little house and pointed proudly.

The house had three wooden sides, and a fourth side

made of wire like the fences. The wire side had a small open door in it, and enclosing the entire house was a big dog kennel with a roof. But there wasn't a dog in it, and my nose told me there never had been. I would be the first!

"She'll be safe in here," the man said. "The wire roof will keep off any flying predators— there are hawks and owls around."

"Let's put her crate in and open it up," Mom suggested.

I watched alertly as Nose-Hair Man opened up the gate of the kennel, because my nose had picked up the scent of chicken treats, and I am very interested in chicken. Mom put Stinkerbelle's crate inside and slipped open its door. Then she came out, and the man shut and latched the kennel gate.

We watched. The skunk did not stir.

"She's scared," Maggie Rose said softly.

"She's right to be cautious in a new environment," said Dad.

"We haven't fed her yet this morning, so she'll probably come out to get some food," Mom told my girl.

"We put some berries and vegetables and a little bit of cooked chicken in her tray, inside the house," Nose-Hair Man said. My ears perked up when he said "chicken."

Mom nodded. "A nice balanced meal."

We watched some more. Nothing happened. I yawned, not understanding any of this.

"This is boring," Bryan complained. "Hey, look, goats! Can we pet them?"

Nose-Hair Man nodded. "That's the petting area."

"Go ahead. Craig, will you go with him?"

Mom said. "Maggie Rose, how about you? Don't you want to see the goats?"

My girl nodded. "But I want to make sure Stinkerbelle's okay first," she explained.

"That's my game warden girl," Dad said.

The boys left. I watched them go, and looked up at my girl to see what was happening now. Was I the only one who knew about the chicken?

It seemed that we were all still watching my skunk friend. But she wasn't doing much. Was she taking a nap inside her crate?

If we were supposed to play with the skunk, I would have to be let inside. And if that's what everyone wanted, maybe I'd get some chicken out of it.

I went to the kennel gate and pawed at it. I looked up at Maggie Rose.

13

Lily should go into the cage with Stinker-belle!" Maggie Rose exclaimed. I heard my name and figured she was talking about letting me play with my friend. I licked her knee to show her that I loved how she always understood what I needed.

"Well, I don't know. . . ." Nose-Hair Man replied doubtfully.

"They're friends," my girl told him.

"See, now that the skunk is here, the critter's safety is my responsibility. If I put a dog in there and something happens, I get in a lot of trouble."

"Lily is something of an ambassador at our rescue," Mom explained. "She greets almost every animal who stays with us. It's amazing how she helps them calm down. She's been inside a kennel with the skunk every day. My daughter is right—Lily probably will help the skunk feel at home here."

"It's against the rules," the man said, his nose hair twitching.

I was getting impatient. I barked and Stinkerbelle reacted by sticking her face out of her crate and gazing at me. Nearly all animals wish they could bark like a dog.

"See? She wants Lily to help her feel better!"

"It doesn't look like the food is luring the skunk out, but she's okay with the dog," Dad observed reasonably.

"She gets hungry enough, she'll come out," Nose-Hair drawled.

"But that's not right," Maggie Rose argued. "Then she'll be scared *and* hungry."

The man scratched at the hair under his nose, and I found myself sitting and itching at my ear in response. "You do make yourself a good point there, young lady." He sighed. "Well, I guess it's worth a shot." The man unlatched the gate and I trotted inside.

I looked around with interest. There was a hollow log along the back, and over in the little house I could smell a bowl full of food—the chicken!—and another with water.

I stuck my head into the crate. There was Stinkerbelle, who had backed up and was crouched low to the ground, not moving.

I wagged at her so that she'd know this was a safe place to be. She lifted her head. I wagged some more.

Then I turned around to check out the bowls in the little house.

After a moment, I heard a very soft rustling behind me. Stinkerbelle was following. When I stuck my head in the open doorway to the little house, she brushed right past me and put her nose next to mine in the food bowl.

"Well, I'll be," Nose-Hair Man said softly.

I made room for her. She took up a piece of apple and crunched it. She could have the apples. That was fine with me. I was more interested in the pieces of chicken. I snapped them up and then lapped at a drink.

"Dad, isn't the skunk going to be lonely without Lily?" Maggie Rose asked softly.

"I don't think so," Dad said. "Skunks are solitary animals. They live alone. Sometimes when it's very cold, they'll find a burrow with other skunks inside and huddle up, but that's pretty rare. Most of the time they're by themselves. It's natural for them."

The skunk ate a little more. Then she moved over to the water dish and drank, too.

She lifted up her head with water dripping off her muzzle. I licked it off for her. Outside of the cage, Nose-Hair Man whistled softly.

"So they're not like the prairie dogs," Maggie Rose said.

"That's right," Dad agreed. "A prairie dog wouldn't be happy all by itself. They need to be in a group."

"A coterie," Maggie Rose said.

"You got it. But skunks are different."

Then the skunk turned her back on me and went over to one end of the hollow log. She poked her nose inside it. Then, slowly, she climbed inside.

I peeked into the hole in the log. At first all I could see was the skunk's rump. But then there was a rustling noise and the skunk turned herself around. Her little black face with her shiny eyes peered out at me.

The skunk sniffed my nose. I pulled my head back out and looked at Maggie Rose. Stinkerbelle had decided to play Hide-in-a-Log, and I'd done Find-the-Skunk. But Stinkerbelle didn't want to come out or play anything else. She seemed content to curl up in her dark, quiet spot.

Now what?

There was much I did not understand. But I did see that I was in a dog kennel with a skunk, and that my girl and her family and a man with nose hair were all on the other side of the fence.

"Want to come out, Lily?" Maggie Rose asked softly.

Nose-Hair opened the gate, and I decided it was time for me to go back to my girl.

Stinkerbelle did not follow. When I went through the open gate, it was shut behind me. What were we doing? What about my skunk friend? Wasn't she coming back to Work with us?

Maggie Rose knelt and looked deeply into my eyes. "We have to go now, Lily. You did a good job taking care of Stinkerbelle the skunk, but this is where she lives now. We have to say goodbye."

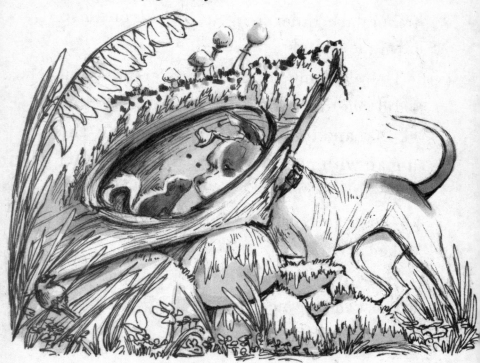

I wagged. I didn't understand much, but I'd heard my friend's name, and I thought that the quiet, solemn way my girl was gazing at me delivered a clear message. When she patted her leg, I fell in step behind her. We were leaving Stinkerbelle behind.

"Craig! Bryan! Time to go!" Mom called.

When we reached the car and Maggie Rose slid into her seat, I hesitated, gazing back at the dog kennel. For just a moment, I thought I saw my friend's nose come out for one last look, but I could not be sure.

I jumped into my girl's lap and thought about all that had just happened. I was starting to understand that I would meet a lot of animals at Work. I would make friends with them and play with them. Some of them, like Casey, would stay. And some would go to new families or new places to live.

That was what the skunk was doing. The small house was her new place to live.

It was a good home. The skunk had food to eat and water to drink and a cozy place to nap. She didn't have anyone to play with, but she actually didn't really *like* playing with other animals, not even a dog—and there is no creature more fun to play with than a dog.

I would miss Stinkerbelle. But the skunk was in her new home, and I was with my girl.

We were both where we were supposed to be.

MORE ABOUT SKUNKS

Skunks are nocturnal. They are active at night and sleep during the day.

Skunks will eat almost anything, but their favorite food is insects and grubs. They will also eat small rodents, frogs, worms, birds' eggs, berries, mushrooms, bees, and wasps.

Skunks sometimes hunt venomous snakes. The venom does not hurt them.

Stinkerbelle is a striped skunk. The Latin name for this animal is *Mephitis mephitis,* which basically means "stinky stinky."

A group of skunks is called a surfeit.

Skunks usually make their dens in hollow logs or trees, brush piles, or inside the burrows of other animals. Sometimes they move in under porches or into abandoned buildings.

Skunks will spray only if they feel cornered or think that their babies are being threatened. You can usually stop a skunk from spraying by backing away and leaving it alone.

Skunks will warn before spraying by stamping their front feet, growling, spitting, and shaking their tails. The spotted skunk does a warning "dance" that looks like a handstand, in which it stands on its front feet and lifts its back legs into the air.

Skunks can spray up to ten or twelve feet. Their spray can be smelled a mile away.

If your pet gets sprayed by a skunk, keep it outside if possible. Don't wash your pet with tomato juice; that won't do anything to get rid of the smell. Pet stores sell special shampoos that can help get skunk spray out of fur. You can also use a mixture of hydrogen peroxide and baking soda, maybe with a little dish soap added. Keep this mixture away from your pet's eyes and scrub and rinse as well as you can. The smell will fade in a few days.

ABOUT THE AUTHOR

Ute Ville

W. BRUCE CAMERON is the *New York Times* bestselling author of *A Dog's Purpose, A Dog's Journey, A Dog's Way Home, A Dog's Promise,* the Puppy Tales books for young readers, and the Lily to the Rescue chapter books. He lives in California.

brucecameronbooks.com

Introducing
BruceCameronKidsBooks.com
the brand new hub for
W. Bruce Cameron's
bestselling adventure tales

Check out fun videos and downloadable
activities paw-fect for the whole family!

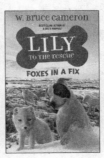